IF MORTALS KNEW...

POWERFUL INSIGHTS FROM THE AFTERLIFE

BY

JOHN L. MCKAY

IF MORTALS KNEW...Powerful Insights from the Afterlife

Copyright ©2023 by John L. McKay and Choiceful Life Publishing, LLC. All rights reserved.

Printed in the United States of America. No part of this book may be used or reproduced in any manner whatsoever without written permission from the author.

Layout and Design: Variance Author Services
www.varianceauthorservices.com
Cover Art: Alex_82

If Mortals Knew...

Powerful Insights from the Afterlife

By

John L. McKay

ACKNOWLEDGMENTS

My heartfelt gratitude to those whose encouragement and support helped this book come to fruition:

To my wonderful pre-readers – thank you so much for your time, effort and great suggestions:

- Suzanne and Tim Hawker
- Ken Holmen
- Nick Neuhausel
- Joe Simonet
- Daniel Stodtmeister and Sarah Thompson
- Jacob and Jessica Stodtmeister

Jenni, Maddie and Katelyn – your initial reaction helped motivate me. To all of you and your siblings mentioned above, as well as Erika, Garima, Claire, Justin, Garrett, Paige, and Kolby – you all inspire and support me in ways for which I am forever grateful. Thank you!

Thanks to my editor Tim Schulte, for your partnership, guidance and thoughtful recommendations; and Boyd Ware and Steve Stay for answering my novice questions about the world of publishing.

A *very* special thanks goes to my sweetheart, Janet. You patiently sat through each reading (many times!) going way above and beyond. You selflessly took so much time and provided thoughtful input rewrite after rewrite. Thank you not only for your ongoing encouragement and support, but for your suggestions that made this a much better book, and that hopefully are helping me be a better man.

Dedicated to those special Angels that have preceded me in this great adventure:

Mom, Dad and Mark

Chapter One

The last thing Jeffrey Morris expected to do today was to die.

In fact, it was the furthest thing from his mind.

Jeff and his best friend Nick Colter were tucked into a two-man canoe on the Snake River in Wyoming, excited to face their first rapids. Earlier that morning they'd been taught with a group of other novice boaters how to keep the canoe pointing down river, how to sync their efforts to steer in the direction they wanted, and more importantly, what to do and not do to simply stay upright. Once they got the basics down, they headed out, launching just below Jackson Lake damn.

The initial, gentle stretch of the river gave them time to get a feel for the boat and work together before facing the water's challenges. Nick, the much taller and larger of the two, was in the back. He was a big enough guy that when he first got in the boat, it practically lifted the bow out of the water. As Jeffrey crawled in, it lowered it some and they both laughed at the disparity. Jeff had teased Nick that he'd be lucky to get his paddle in the water.

Both rowers were kneeling, and Jeff's legs were already starting to hurt. Knee pads lightened the discomfort a bit and he'd been assured that his appendages would numb up eventually. After about twenty minutes of rowing, his arms and shoulders were aching. Jeff was sure they would fall off, but gradually they began to loosen up and settle into the task at hand. That gave him hope that his legs would be next to get on board. He tried sitting up high, then lowering on his haunches every few minutes to spread the discomfort as he adjusted.

It was a beautiful spring morning. For Jeff and his equally outdoor-loving buddy, aches and pains were outweighed by the glory of nature surrounding them. They saw countless shades of green amongst the tall trees, bushes and grass; wildflowers of all kinds dotting the shoreline, sunlight dancing in patterns off the river, and brief glimpses of the jagged Tetons in the distance. They'd even spotted a moose at the last bend lazily drinking, giving them only a brief glance as it quickly determined they were no threat. The temperature was just right, and the water was high from spring runoff, which would add power to the rapids. It was all in all, a perfect day.

As they approached their first whitewater, Jeff reviewed in his mind the basic guidelines they'd been given for this initial, critical part of their adventure.

"You will all likely tip over at some point," the guide had warned. *"In fact, count on it. When you do, hold onto your paddle. That's your first responsibility. You're not going to get much farther down the river without it, and you've got two full days ahead of you."* Jeff laughed, reliving the scene as the guide emphasized, *"So unless you want to paddle with your hands the whole time, keep a grip on your oar."*

He continued, *"If you tip over, don't panic. Do your best to keep your feet downriver. That will position you to push off rocks and give you the time you need to get your bearings. You might still bounce over some boulders that are under the water and bruise your butt a little, but most of those are smooth from erosion and you can push off the jagged ones above the surface. After you're through the rapids, you'll be able to stand up once you're in a shallow spot, or swim to your boat or the bank. We'll get to you as soon as we can and help you back into your canoe.*

"Logjams are your biggest danger." The guide pointed to what looked like a tiny island in the middle of the river, with large sticks protruding in every direction. *"Avoid those at all costs. The force of the water can push you right under them and you don't come out, so make sure you steer clear,"* he stressed.

Jeff had taken all this in stride. He'd started young as a swimmer and knew he was good enough to handle any water hazards that might come his way. At one point during the training, he saw his buddy Nick impatiently roll his eyes his direction, indicating that he too was anxious to get going. More demonstrations and practice followed, and then finally, they tightened up their life vests and took to the water.

That was all earlier. Seeing their first churning water ahead and focusing on the challenge at hand, Jeff yelled over his shoulder to Nick, "Here it comes. Let's do this!"

Their canoe hit the first rising wave, lifting Jeff, then barreling down into a trough where a blast of cold water splashed over the bow, soaking his shirt and both their lower legs. Up, then down – both men yelling their delight at this nature-made roller coaster. They paddled hard, alternating quickly on both sides to avoid rocks, stay upright and keep pointing forward. It only lasted about thirty seconds, but it felt much longer…and it was awesome!

As they slid into calmer waters, Nick yelled, "Look back." Jeff glanced behind and saw that all but one of the canoes in the group had made the first round. The boat with the older couple had swamped. The two were in the river, sputtering water, but still smiling as one of the guides bringing up the rear paddled over. She helped them turn their canoe upright and held it as they got in. They watched as the couple used the Clorox bottles they'd cut in half and secured with a rope to the boat, to bail out the excess water.

Jeff and Nick were laughing, grateful that they were at least dryer than the two who had been dunked. They too scooped out as much of the water from the bottom of their canoe as they were able.

"That was incredible!" Jeff yelled. "And the guide said they're going to get bigger!"

The excitement of the rapids was tempered by long stretches of slow, even paddling with the current doing much of the work. The joyful boaters soaked in the beauty surrounding them. As promised, the next three sets of rapids were even more thrilling, each a little longer than the one before. The two enthusiasts paddled furiously, laughing and yelling all the way, managing to stay upright while two other boats – one in front and one behind them – flipped over, their crews quickly rescued by their supportive guides.

After the fourth stretch of whitewater, and everyone was back in their boats and ready to go, the lead guide cautioned them, yelling, "Hey everyone! Our last set of rapids for the day is coming up around the bend. It's the biggest one yet, so have fun, but be careful. After that, we'll pull out of the river and have dinner at the camp. You're all doing great."

"How amazing is this?" Jeff exclaimed to Nick. "Camp is set up for us, dinner all ready and we have a warm, dry place to sleep. It doesn't get any better than this."

Nick nodded, then nudged his buddy with the end of his oar, "Let's hit these next rapids as hard as we can. I still think we can go faster." Jeff readily agreed and started rowing harder than he had all day as he spotted the churning water ahead. Nick paddled quickly behind him.

As they hit the first wave, the front of the boat seemed to shoot straight up. Jeff's momentum thrust him forward. He lost his balance and slammed his chin on the bow. He tried to right himself, but as the canoe dipped back down, he was left briefly suspended in the air. He came down at an angle, hitting the edge of the canoe hard, cutting his hand and slamming his rib cage against the side. For a moment he was unable to breathe, the wind knocked out of him. He instinctively dropped his paddle and grabbed the side of the canoe to steady himself, but as the bow hit the next wave, his face again planted hard on the edge of the canoe, cutting his lip. He tried desperately to get control. It was then he noticed his paddle bounding off a wave nearby.

I have to grab that! Jeff thought to himself. As he reached as far out as he could, the front of the canoe glanced off of a rock, flipping the entire boat up and sideways. He found himself suddenly flying through the air, then disappearing under the freezing water.

Jeff's life vest pushed him quickly to the surface, where he spluttered and coughed, his ribs aching. Though the water was extremely cold, and in spite of the pain, he knew he was alright. He turned to look for Nick and saw him about ten feet to his left. Nick saw him at the same time. They paused a few seconds, then both started laughing.

"That wasn't our best moment," Jeff exclaimed as he started paddling toward his friend, both being carried quickly down river.

Nick's laughter halted. "Man, your mouth is bleeding!"

Jeff reached up and felt his lip, then looked at his fingers and saw blood mixed with the water. He checked and assured himself that his teeth were intact. He'd hit the boat hard and suspected he'd feel it big-time tonight. His hand had a small gash on it but didn't hurt much because of the cold water. He shook his head. He couldn't really think about his injuries right then. They had to get back to the boat.

"Feet front!" Jeff yelled, remembering the guide's instruction, but Nick was already well-positioned. It was Jeff who was facing sideways, his torso leading his legs down river. With some effort, he righted himself and got his feet ahead of him. That was when he spotted a large pile of logs in the water just ahead.

"Logjam!" he yelled.

"I see it." Nick responded.

Whoa, that's wide, he thought, and he was positioned right in the middle of it. With only a second to decide, knowing that Nick was to his left, Jeff went right, swimming hard to get around the gnarly mess. Suddenly, their canoe struck his head from the right. He'd been thrown ahead of their boat, and it was just now catching up. As Jeff pulled back in surprise, it moved past and blocked his way. He tried to push it aside, anxious to go forward, but it moved along with him, both being swept by the current.

Suddenly, the front of the canoe hit a rock, flipping it to the right, torquing the back end up and behind Jeff. That put him between the canoe and the jam, forcing him closer to the huge pile of limbs. Knowing he was about to hit, Jeff strained to turn himself so that he might grab some higher limbs at the front and pull himself out, but the canoe and the force of the water drove him right into the waiting sticks and under the jam.

Everything around Jeff's head was now a swirl of sharp sticks and cold, churning water. One unbending limb dug into his face. The belt on his life vest caught on another thick branch which trapped his torso below the surface, with his head under the water. Jeff kicked hard, but another stick skewered his right calf causing him to wince in pain. He hadn't taken a very deep breath before hitting the jam and knew he only had seconds to pull himself out.

Reaching up, he grabbed the logs and pulled with all his might. Nothing happened. He struggled harder, thrashed, tried to pull himself free, but it seemed he only went deeper. This went on and on and Jeff was desperate. He was trapped, running out of air, out of energy and out of time. His lungs were burning. He had to breathe. He sensed he was losing consciousness. One more frantic pull, but nothing. With his last bit of energy, Jeff instinctively screamed, hoping against reason that he'd be heard and rescued, then took in a deep breath. He simply had to. But it wasn't the air he desperately needed. He felt his lungs fill with cold water…and then he relaxed.

He wasn't sure how long it had been, but Jeff suddenly found himself on top of the logjam. He couldn't believe it. He'd made it! What a relief, but how?! Did the logs give way? Did the current somehow toss him up here? It didn't matter – he was alive! He felt instant relief. The searing pain was gone – his face and legs weren't hurting, his lungs seemed okay. It was as if none of this terrifying experience had even happened. Maybe he'd blacked out and dreamt part of this, yet he felt entirely awake and fine – more than fine.

Jeff saw the guide's canoe with both leaders coming toward the jam to help him. He yelled over the rushing water that he was okay – that they should make sure Nick was alright, signaling in his direction. They ignored him, pulled close to where he was standing, and started grabbing at Jeff's canoe to push it aside.

"I'm telling you I'm fine," Jeff yelled. "Go find Nick!" But they continued to ignore him.

Just then, Jeff spotted Nick out of the corner of his eye. He was standing on the other end of the logjam. He was so happy to see him, relieved that they both were okay.

"Wow, that was close!" Jeff yelled to his friend. "I seriously thought I was a goner!"

But Nick didn't look over. He was staring into the water and had a very troubled look on his face. Jeff couldn't see what his friend was looking at, but instinctively glanced down in front of his own feet and saw something that startled him. There was what looked like a head of hair just below the surface next to where he was standing. His heart dropped. Had someone else been caught in the same logjam? Was it a member of their group? He didn't recognize the hair and couldn't see the face. He turned to yell at Nick, to call him over, but saw that two men dressed in white were standing there talking to him.

Odd that paramedics made it here so quickly, Jeff thought. "Hey, there's a guy in the water over here who needs your help," he yelled to the strangers. "You need to hurry!"

They calmly looked over, then back at Nick, engaging him in earnest conversation. Jeff was confused by their lack of urgency. He wanted to make his way over to his friend, but something seemed to keep him riveted there. He looked down again at the body in the water and watched as one of the guides frantically used a large Bowie knife to cut off the life vest. Then he and two others that had arrived started pulling hard to free the body. Jeff thought he should probably be scared. He was about to see what he was sure was a fresh corpse. Instead, he was entirely at peace, more curious than afraid. He wondered if perhaps it was just profound relief from having avoided death. He glanced over at Nick, wanting him to come witness this strange event with him.

Nick was still having a serious conversation with the two men and looked very troubled. *They should lay off him*, Jeff thought. *We just went through a terrifying experience.*

And then the most remarkable thing happened. One of the men put his hand on Nick's shoulder. Nick seemed to relax, looked over at Jeff, started to say something, and then disappeared. Nick was gone!

Before he could comprehend what he'd just witnessed, Jeff saw Nick sit up in the middle of one of the canoes that had pulled up on the far side. He was coughing, spluttering, gasping for air, and then heaved up a bunch of water. The men in the canoe were attending to him, patting his back, then made him lie down again. The paramedics on the logjam had vanished.

Jeff shook his head. *I must have bumped it harder than I thought. I'm seeing things. One moment Nick's on the logjam, the next he's back in the boat. And those paramedics got here far too quickly. What's going on?!*

He was confused by everything that was happening and yet, deep down, instead of panic, he was feeling more and more at peace. *Here I'm standing over a dead body, I almost died myself, and yet I'm completely calm.*

Suddenly, Jeffrey knew who was trapped beneath the logjam, and yet there was no fear, no sadness, just serenity. He watched as they struggled to free his body, touched by their efforts and concern. It took time, but the team of guides finally pulled his lifeless body into one of the waiting boats, where they quickly started chest compressions and mouth-to-mouth resuscitation.

Jeff had left the logjam and was now hovering directly over the boat, more fascinated by what he saw below, than that he was actually floating.

That's me, he thought, *but not really. The real me is up here.* Jeff tried to let them know he was okay – more than okay. He actually wanted them to leave him alone. A moment ago, he'd been immersed in water. Now he was immersed in the most incredible feeling of peace and he didn't want to be brought back. He finally gave up trying, unable to communicate with any of those working on him.

The lead guide anxiously reminded the others that, because of the effects of cold water on the body, they shouldn't give up, so their efforts continued for what seemed like a long time. Finally, it was clear that Jeff was dead. They stopped trying to save him, visibly shaken by what had happened. One put his hand on Jeff's forehead and bowed his head. One swore, angry and frustrated that there was nothing more they could do. Another was wiping away tears as he fought to not break down.

Wow, I've just died, Jeff thought. Most remarkable was how pleasant it was. He had to struggle to even remember that a short time ago he'd been in pain, panic and fighting for his life. Then in an instant, he was at peace, feeling joy that moments ago was beyond his comprehension. Death had been as easy as stepping from one room into another.

Nick sat up again and became aware of what was happening in the nearby boat. He started sobbing, "Don't leave me, man. You fight! You fight, Jeff!" he yelled. He finally saw those working on his friend stop, and sadly acknowledged that they had failed to rescue him. Nick yelled that they should keep trying, but everyone knew that it was no use.

Jeff hovered over his crying friend. *"I'm alright. I promise,"* he assured him, but Nick couldn't hear him, couldn't be consoled.

"He'll be alright," someone close by said.

Jeff turned and saw someone standing next to him. He had dark brown hair, brown eyes, and a warm smile. He was dressed in a long, bright white robe that stopped just above his bare feet. What really caught Jeff's attention was that, even though he looked like a man, his entire body was exuding light. More than light, he seemed to radiate the same peace that Jeffrey was now feeling from head to toe.

"What?" Jeff asked.

"He'll be alright," the being repeated.

"Are you sure?" Then, Jeff felt embarrassed for questioning him.

He nodded. "I'm sure of it. Hello Jeffrey." *He knew his name.*

Jeff paused, not sure how to respond. He felt like he should perhaps drop to his knees. He ventured another question. "I don't know if I'm supposed to ask you this, but…are you an angel?"

The man smiled. "You can call me that…for now. I'm here to bring you home."

"Home?"

Without answering, Angel turned and stepped in the other direction. Jeff instinctively followed. Then he paused. *What about my brother, Jake? Is he going to be okay?* he thought to himself.

As if sensing his thoughts, the angel turned and said, "Your loved ones will be alright. Come with me."

Jeffrey nodded. A light that had been growing behind the heavenly messenger grew even brighter as they both faced it. For a second, it seemed he shouldn't look at it. He'd been taught as a child not to stare at the sun because it would hurt his eyes, and this was so much brighter. Yet he felt – he knew – he would be safe looking at it. The light now appeared to be swirling in waves, creating a circular pattern that formed a tunnel. Something inside the tunnel seemed to beckon him forward. He turned to look one more time at Nick, once more at his own lifeless body, then turned back to Angel.

Angel put his hand on Jeff's shoulder. He could feel it. He could actually feel an angel touching him. At that moment, it seemed the most natural thing in the world…or…out of it, Jeff thought to himself.

So, this is what death is. The thought from earlier came back to him. *It's as easy as stepping into another room.*

Together they walked forward.

Chapter Two

As Jeff and Angel stepped from the tunnel, Jeff was enveloped in a myriad of powerful emotions. He had just relived his entire life – not just viewed it, not just seen highlights of it, but had somehow emotionally experienced everything from birth to his drowning.

He had watched and felt with tender fascination what it was like to come into the world as a baby, to learn to walk and talk, and to have grown up with his parents and younger brother, Jake. He'd seen friends, teachers and coworkers, some he'd completely forgotten. There were happy memories, sad ones, exciting moments and proud ones. There were some painful experiences and some that were embarrassing, especially with Angel by his side. He hoped that his heavenly guide might somehow miss seeing those.

Most touching was seeing his sweet mother and feeling her love and support. Oh, how he had missed her. He wanted to somehow slow down his life's instant replay, so he could focus on his mom, but instinctively knew they had to keep moving forward. He was surprised at how many pleasant memories there were with his dad, all before mom's death, before dad had started drinking heavily and lashing out at him and Jake. Jeff had grown tough enough to handle it, but he would never forgive his dad for hurting his younger brother. He didn't want to think of his father ever again – ugly memories he hoped he could leave behind, but all of it was now fresh.

Something that mystified him in this life review was that he experienced all twenty-one-plus years in a matter of minutes. Even the term "minutes" didn't seem to apply. Time had somehow folded over itself, so that he comprehended all those memories at once. It was quite overwhelming. He stopped to take a deep breath.

A breath? Yes, he was actually breathing. He hadn't thought before of dead people breathing. Is that what he was – a dead person? No, he actually felt more alive now than he had on Earth. His senses were all firing on maximum – and yes, he was *breathing*.

As Jeff looked around, he saw he had landed in what appeared to be an enormous white room or space. "White" didn't even describe it. It was more like he was standing on and surrounded by extremely bright light that encased them both. As intense as it was, like the tunnel opening, it wasn't hard to look at and even deepened that wonderful, underlying feeling of peace.

"Welcome to Paradise," said Angel. "You can ask me anything. That's one of the reasons I'm here for you. But first…"

Angel didn't get to finish.

"Jeffrey!"

Jeff looked in the direction of the voice. He saw a bright flash of light and a portal opening in the middle of the air. To his astonishment, his mother stepped through the light. Her arms were extended, and tears were flowing freely. She ran to him, swept him up in her arms and held him close.

"Mom!" Jeff hugged her tightly, crying. "Mom, you're here! You're really here! I've missed you! I've missed you so much!"

They continued hugging and crying joyously together, not saying anything – just holding each other in an expression of pure love. As Jeff finally pulled back to look at her, he realized she was the younger version of his mother he'd just seen in the tunnel – about the age when he was born, more beautiful than ever, beaming with joy.

He hugged her tightly once again. This time, as she held him, she spoke softly in his ear, "My dearest boy, I was completely free of the pain the moment I passed on." Jeff began to weep uncontrollably. "In fact, not only was I pain free, but I also experienced the most remarkable joy I've ever felt, as I know you just did. I was filled with light and complete healing. I know you've worried about that all these years, my sweet boy, but please know that I couldn't remember that pain right now if I tried."

Jeff couldn't speak. He was feeling such a profound release of emotions he had bottled up all these years. It had killed him many times over to think that his dear mother had suffered so much from that ugly cancer. Many times, he'd cried out angrily at God, wondering why He had allowed his mother to suffer when she'd been such an innocent, selfless, loving woman. Yet, in the blink of an eye with this reunion, all the pain he'd felt was swallowed up in relief and joy.

"I was told you were coming. I was surprised that it happened so soon – you're so young. But there's a reason for everything, my son. We have all the time in the universe to catch up, but first I want you to meet some people. Other loved ones have come to greet you."

Jeff's mother gestured behind her. Another flash of light and two people stepped out. Though he hadn't known them on Earth, he recognized his grandparents from a photo his mom had kept by her bed. They too each gave him a warm, loving embrace.

"Hey Jeffrey, welcome! Loved watching your football games," his grandpa said. "You were one heck of a defensive back."

"You saw my games?" Jeff asked, surprised at this revelation. "You mean from here?"

"Love transcends all boundaries. The veil between the spirit world and Earth is very thin when it comes to a family's love and support. And anyway," grandpa paused for effect, nudging Jeff with his elbow, "nothing is going to keep me away from a good football game – especially one of yours!"

Grandma smiled and added, "Do you think that anything in this universe could keep us away from our grandchildren? We were there all along."

More ancestors, almost all he didn't know, arrived in flashes of light. As they greeted him, his mother clarified who they were and their relationship to him. Each then shared something he or she appreciated about Jeffrey from moments they witnessed or a talent or ability he'd demonstrated on Earth. It reminded him of when there was a birthday in his family. His mother would insist on going around the table after a special dinner and having everyone say something in tribute to the person celebrating. He'd just reviewed those moments in the tunnel, warming his heart as he felt the love expressed by his family.

A few of his relatives talked about challenges he faced and assured him they had been particularly close during those times. Jeff was touched and surprised by their first-hand knowledge of key events in his life. He had no idea so much support had been there, especially at those times when he was struggling.

During the reunion, Jeff's mother stood by his side holding and sometimes stroking his hand. She let go only long enough for her son to exchange hugs with other loved ones.

At one point, Jeff was talking with his favorite uncle, Dave. "Big D," as Jeff had called his very tall uncle, had died around the same time as his mother. He was telling him he appreciated that Jeffrey had made a point of reaching out to others – "the underdogs", as Big D described them – helping them feel accepted. He was thanking his uncle when he saw a large flash of light, then something running toward him.

"Harley! Arnie!" He immediately recognized the dogs he'd had at different times in his young life – now together. Harley was a beautiful golden retriever, Arnie a huge St. Bernard.

Arnie reached Jeff first and leapt right into his arms, knocking him on his back. He lay there with Arnie standing over him licking his face, Harley joining in. Jeff laughed out loud with tears flowing, everyone else smiling at the joyous scene.

"They're the best of friends," Angel said. "I think they were almost as excited to see you as your mom was."

"These were two of my best friends at different times in my life," Jeff explained. "I can't believe they're here, and together!"

"It wouldn't be much of a paradise without *all* of our loved ones," responded Angel.

The joyous reunion went on for some time. Slowly, the well-wishers departed leaving just Jeff, his mother, Harley, Arnie, and Angel. Jeff was sitting on a floor of light, Harley's head on one leg, Arnie's on the other, with Jeff scratching both while talking to his mother and Angel standing over them.

"I keep saying it, but this is amazing," Jeff exclaimed, shaking his head. "To see you, mom, to have these two back and to learn first-hand that I have so many family members is incredible. I didn't know most of them, yet every single one was able to tell me something about my life – and not just general stuff, they gave me details. I wish I'd known so many people were watching over me. I think it would have made life easier."

"There's a delicate balance that needs to be maintained to maximize our learning during our earthly experience – what you should and shouldn't know, as well as when, that provides the greatest potential for growth," Angel explained. "We'll explore that together. For now, just be present with your mother and get caught up. You have a lot to discuss. I'll find you when you're ready and answer your questions. We'll reflect and learn from what you've already experienced since your mortal death and then discuss what's next."

"What's next?" Jeffrey was curious to know what was coming. "Sounds intriguing. How will you know when I'm ready?"

"I'll know. I'll see you then. You two enjoy getting caught up."

Jeff's mom started leading him toward an open portal.

"Wait!" Jeffrey turned back. "You said I'd be learning from my death and experiences here. Something in the way you said it made it sound like I'm going back to school. Say it isn't so," he remarked, only half-jokingly. Sitting in school hadn't exactly been his favorite activity.

"You'll love it," Angel smiled.

Jeffrey immediately somehow knew he would.

Chapter Three

As mother and son stepped arm-in-arm out of another tunnel, Jeff noticed they were standing on a hill, overlooking something that took his breath away. He saw in a panoramic view the world of spirits – the most beautiful place he'd ever seen or could have imagined. Jeffrey stood frozen in awe.

In contrast to the stark space they had just left, here was a stunning, multi-colored, brightly lit town, nestled at the base of towering mountains with a beautiful, deep-blue lake to his right. The homes were made of different shaped stones, each nestled into lush gardens – a village of charming English cottages that reminded him of a Kincaid painting. Flowers of all varieties bloomed perfectly, including colors he didn't recognize. As he looked closer at nearby blossoms, he saw that the petals were vibrant, because they were lit from within. In fact, everything was. Every stone, flower, tree – all appeared to exude their own light.

He stepped up to examine a flower more closely.

"Go ahead and pick it," his mother offered.

Jeff hesitated, not wanting to disturb something so beautiful, then slowly reached out to pluck the most perfect yellow rose he'd ever seen. As he extended his arm, it turned into a luxurious, deep red rose – his favorite color. Jeffrey smiled at his mom, then back at the flower that seemed to be reacting to him. He hesitated again, not wanting to disrupt something so amazing, so perfect, so…alive.

"It's alright," his mother encouraged. "You can't hurt it."

Jeffrey expected to have to pull or twist the rose, but it came off easily at his touch. At the same moment, there was a small flash of light on the end of the stem and a new rose quickly blossomed where he'd picked the old one, this time a glowing orange. Jeff laughed in surprise and delight.

He held the red rose to his nose. The fragrance was wonderful. He held it there for several moments, just breathing it in. When he finally moved it away from his face, the rose broke up into dozens of little lights that flew around in circles like brilliant fireflies. They gathered and flew past the new orange rose, landing and absorbing into the ground. The dirt, which had its own light, grew brighter for a moment as the little starlings entered, pushing light up through the stems of the flowers nearby.

"This is unbelievable!" Jeffrey exclaimed.

"That's how I felt the first time I saw all of this. I remember looking forward to sharing it with you and Jake, and now you're here," she smiled, squeezing Jeffrey's hand. "We've just come from a spirit arrival area of sorts. This view of the world of spirits is initially kept from everyone who dies, because it would be too distracting. God lets us focus first on family, reconnecting with those who have passed on before, and meeting those from earlier generations. After that reunion, we choose where we reside, either a small town or a larger city – all different types, shapes and sizes, depending on where we will be happiest. This scene reminded me of an English countryside, so I chose to live here. Of course, regardless of the surroundings, being together again with our loved ones brings the greatest joy." She continued squeezing Jeffrey's hand.

"I could stand here forever," Jeff sighed. "Is this heaven?"

"No, this is Paradise, the spirit world," his mother answered. "Heaven comes later and is apparently even more glorious, though that's hard to imagine. Let me show you my home."

They started down the hill. As they approached the town, Jeff realized he was barefoot, walking on a smooth path that wound through a well-groomed, rich green lawn. The grass shone, as well, each blade lit from within. He noticed every possible shade of green around him, from nearby bushes to trees in the distance. Mixed in with the green trees were others with multi-colored leaves that looked like splendid autumn foliage on Earth. It was as though spring and fall were happening at the same time, yet more vividly because of each radiating leaf.

Jeff noticed the nearby mountains were covered with beautiful pines. He looked closer and could see details of each pinecone, each seed a different shade of brown, pulsating with light.

Startled by this sudden close-up view, he quickly glanced back down at his feet, then back to the pinecones, he now estimated to be miles away. Jeff could see details extremely well, including tiny beads of water on a blade of grass below him and separate needles on a tree in the distance.

He shook his head, realizing that he was seeing both closeup and far away – *really* far away. He could focus his attention on any one thing – near, far or anywhere in between – and see it clearly. It seemed as though it should be overwhelming, but it was the most natural thing in the world…in this world anyway. The intense combination of sights, sounds, scents, feelings, as well as the ability to see up close or far away would have blown a fuse on Earth if he'd had one. But here, it seemed to come naturally.

"I take it you know I'm seeing things close up and far away, right?" Jeffrey asked his mom.

"Without the limitations of your earthly body, you'll be astounded at what you can do here," his mother declared.

As they continued their walk, Jeffrey started noticing other spirits. Two were walking together, holding hands on a path close by, others gathered laughing and talking with each other. A few sitting on a front porch smiled and nodded their direction, and many were gathered in what looked to be some sort of event in a park, as a group of children played nearby. Every race imaginable was here, each exuding his or her own light. He sensed there were spirits here from every generation and every nation on Earth, living together peaceably in an atmosphere of light and love. Jeff focused on another group of spirits visiting with each other. One said something that made the others laugh and for a moment the light amongst them appeared to glow a little brighter.

Rounding a corner, Jeff spotted another quaint town that seemed several miles away and, beyond that, a city with tall, glistening buildings. It was all here. He focused for a moment on a pretty little cottage that caught his eye in the town beyond. He couldn't see a door, just large windows that were simply openings in the beautiful granite, but with no glass. Suddenly, what seemed to be living stones that made up the home opened, creating a doorway. A woman stepped out. She looked directly at Jeff and gave him a warm smile, as if to personally welcome him.

Jeff was startled. His vision immediately pulled back to where he was standing, embarrassed that he might have intruded on the woman's privacy yet astounded at what he'd seen and felt at a distance.

"She wanted to welcome you. You're fine," explained his mother.

"Amazing!" Jeff replied. "It's all just so amazing!"

Just then, Jeff felt something large rub up against the back of his leg. It about knocked him over. Thinking it was Arnie or Harley, he looked behind and noticed a large wolf.

"Whoa!" Jeff quickly jumped back.

His mother laughed. "It's okay. He wants you to scratch behind his ears."

"You're kidding, right? Isn't that a wolf?!"

"It is. Give it a try," mom nudged.

Jeff very slowly reached down and lightly touched the wolf. Then, feeling he was safe, scratched behind his ears, then down his neck and back. It was so powerful, so strong and yet gentle. Finally, the large animal bounded off. A little lamb ran up beside him and the two walked off, side by side.

"A little shameless advertising for the new arrivals," Jeff's mother chuckled, "but it does make a point."

Jeff had been in church enough to get the reference from Isaiah. He and his mom looked at each other, then started laughing.

"This is going to take some getting used to…but I love it!"

"Here we are. I'll show you your home next. I've designed something I think you'll like, but you can adjust it however you want with just a thought. Let's catch up first in mine," Jeff's mother said. The shining slabs of marble that made up her home created a doorway as they approached and went inside.

Chapter Four

Jeffrey wasn't sure how much time had gone by as he visited with his mom. In fact, there wasn't a sense of time here in the spirit world – no watches or clocks, no cell phones, not even the sun crossing the sky. He didn't have deadlines, nothing he needed to rush to, which allowed him to completely relax and enjoy his mother. When Jeff mentioned how freeing that felt, his mom agreed and added that, at a deeper level, since there was no longer a fear or unconscious awareness of death, there was no ultimate "end" about which they needed to think or worry. She knew first-hand the significance of that from her own prolonged death and exclaimed with a big sigh how liberating it was.

As they visited, Jeff was surprised at what his mother knew about his life, especially the ten years they'd been apart. She pretty much knew everything but had still insisted and delighted in hearing it all from him. They talked first about Jake, then about work, school, sports, dating, friends, challenges, accomplishments, and failures. She didn't react as much as he thought she would when he finally talked about his dad's descent into drunkenness and anger after her death.

"I'm fully aware of it," she said calmly. "We'll talk about that when you're ready."

"I'm ready right now. I can handle it," Jeffrey exclaimed. He suddenly felt bad that he'd pushed back on his mom, especially after such a wonderful reunion.

"Actually, you're not," his mother firmly replied. "Trust me that there will be a better time for that discussion."

"Jeffrey." He heard a voice outside his mother's home. The wall opened up and Angel was standing there. "Hello you two. Jeffrey, do I get to borrow you for a bit?"

Jeff was pleased to see Angel but didn't want to leave his mom. She sensed his reluctance, gave him a hug, then reached up, holding his face in her hands, kissed his forehead and said, "This is meant to be one-on-one, so I'm going to leave you two alone. I'll see you soon. Remember that I'm only a thought away. Always have been. Now I'm going to go visit my sister."

She hugged him again and gave him the most tender look, almost melting him with feelings of love. Then she turned and disappeared in a flash of light.

∞∞∞

"Good to see you again, my friend! I'd ask how your reunion with your mom went, but your beaming face speaks volumes. Are you ready to continue our adventure?"

"Absolutely," said Jeff, happy to be back together with this heavenly being.

"As you and your mom were leaving, you joked about not wanting to go back to school. What was your concern?" Angel asked.

"I just didn't picture a campus here in Paradise," Jeff responded, "and certainly not sitting in a stuffy classroom. I was hoping that was all behind me."

"One of many things we'll explore together is our assumptions; what we might be locked into and how some of our *thought habits* can impact our growth," Angel explained. "Notice how quickly you tied learning to a traditional classroom. School buildings as we know them now didn't exist on Earth for centuries, yet people were learning all along, right?"

"I guess so," Jeffrey conceded. "I hadn't thought of it that way. But," he quickly added, not wanting to appear wrong, "I think that would be expected from someone who lived when I did."

Sensing his defensiveness, Angel replied, "Don't make yourself wrong or even right as we explore various topics. Just stay curious. For example, be aware of how you jumped to the assumption of what a classroom is. I think you'll change your mind on that when you experience our approach to learning here. With so many things different here in the spirit world, I'd challenge you to keep your mind open to the possibilities."

"You mentioned a thought habit. What's that?" Jeffrey inquired.

"I'm going to throw that question back at you. What does having a thought habit sound like?"

"Well, when it comes to habits; those are obviously things I've done enough times that I do them without thinking, like brushing my teeth, riding a bike or making my bed in the morning. I guess a thought habit is like that, but in my head – something I've contemplated so many times that thinking it is as natural as my physical habits."

"You're right on track. There are both positive and negative thought habits or mindsets, and of course, some are more serious than others. Connecting learning to a school building isn't too critical. We'll follow up on that in a moment," Angel said smiling. There was something mischievous in his tone that caught Jeffrey's attention as Angel continued.

"Your Uncle Dave mentioned that he appreciated how you tend to quickly think of other's feelings. That's certainly a positive mindset. There are also serious negative thought habits, like someone thinking that they are stupid, worthless or powerless. Those are mindsets that, once truly believed, can be harmful. As different thought habits pop up for you, which they do for all of us, I'll simply mirror them back and we'll explore whether they are mindsets that will help you grow and advance, or some that will get in your way and hold you back. Will that work for you?"

"Absolutely," said Jeff. Normally, if someone tried to correct him, he'd tell them to mind their own business, but he felt such non-judgment from Angel that he felt open to and even curious about examining some of his weaknesses.

"I mentioned a different kind of classroom," Angel went on. "To really make that point, let's go somewhere where we'll learn together, call it our first classroom, but one as different from a typical school as we could possibly get. First, there's a principle you need to understand that you'll see play out as we learn together."

"What's that?" Jeffrey asked.

"Everything on Earth was created spiritually before it was created physically," Angel stated.

Jeffrey nodded, acting like he knew what that meant, but he wasn't sure.

Angel smiled. "You'll understand more about that in a moment. Now for a question. You were pleasantly surprised to see your dogs when they greeted you but didn't seem shocked in general at seeing animals in the spirit world, whether it was Arnie and Harley, a wolf or a lamb. Do you recall ever thinking that you might see animals after your physical death?"

"I remember sitting in church when I was younger and thinking that heaven wouldn't be much of a heaven without my dogs."

"And if there's a place here for dogs, wolves, lambs, cats, horses, and any other animals you might have spotted already, which of God's creations do you think He would exclude from His kingdom?" Angel inquired.

"Well," Jeffrey paused, "mosquitoes come to mind."

That made Angel laugh. "I hadn't thought of mosquitoes before. They'd probably get my vote, as well. But you'll be surprised to know that they are all here. And I mean *all!*"

On that cryptic note, Angel motioned to Jeffrey, and they stepped into an emerging portal.

In an instant, they were in a place that reminded Jeff of a gigantic swamp, but a clean swamp, even glowing. He spotted them immediately.

"Dinosaurs!" he bellowed. "Dinosaurs?! Are those real?!"

There, stretched out in panoramic view, was what looked to be every type of dinosaur imaginable. Jeff stood there with his mouth gaping open.

At his outburst, many of the dinosaurs lifted their heads and glanced over, curious as to who was seeing them for the first time, then went on eating the dense vegetation. It seemed they were used to new arrivals.

"Yes, they're real. Everything was created spiritually before it was created physically," Angel reminded Jeff, "and that includes our prehistoric friends. That means that when they died on Earth, their spirits, what gave them life, moved into this world, just as yours and mine, your mom's, or Harley and Arnie's." He paused for effect. "So, does this qualify as an interesting classroom?"

Jeff stood there stunned. Dinosaurs! He recognized a triceratops, stegosaurus, many tall brachiosauruses, and even a large T-Rex.

"When something, anything is created by Father, it is given a living spirit. When it dies physically, that spirit comes here. Let's get up close," Angel suggested. "They're completely safe and there's lots to see. Once you've had a chance to absorb it, we'll relax and explore some of your questions."

They started on a long path through the swamp, walking amongst a variety of prehistoric animals. At one point, Harley and Arnie bounded up, rubbing up against Jeff's legs. He'd scratch their heads, then they'd run out into the swamp, around the legs of the larger animals and back to Jeff, enjoying their surroundings and clearly delighted to be reunited with their friend. They repeated this over and over as Jeff and Angel observed this amazing living museum that Jeff quickly dubbed *Jurassicland*.

To Jeff, Jurassicland looked like the best Spielberg movie ever, in IMAX 3D-times a thousand, and this was real. As he got over the shock of seeing dinosaurs, he noticed many "modern" animals were also in the mix, including foxes, squirrels, several large bucks, horses, and some lions. All seemed to get along perfectly. Jeff chuckled when he saw a polar bear and ostrich lounging next to each other. The bear looked completely out of place in the swamp but seemed as content as all the animals around it. He also noticed the occasional human spirits walking amongst them and was surprised to spot others in the distance actually riding some dinosaurs.

"Am I seeing what I think I'm seeing?" Jeffrey inquired, nodding toward the riders on their unusual steeds.

"You'll have to come take a ride," Angel said, confirming what Jeff was seeing. "It feels a lot like riding horseback – very relaxing – and the animals are happy to accommodate." Jeffrey just shook his head, wondering what other surprises lay in store.

At one point, Jeff felt something rub up behind him. Harley and Arnie were in front, so he knew it wasn't them. He turned, expecting to see another wolf wanting to be petted. Instead, he was looking directly into the face of a raptor. He could see other raptors close behind.

"Whoa!" Jeff jumped back. He would have fallen if Angel hadn't caught him. Angel started laughing as Jeff righted himself.

"She won't hurt you. Try scratching her head," Angel nudged.

"I'm thinking that I'll be able to do that in, oh, maybe a million years or so," Jeffrey responded warily.

Jeff watched as Angel petted and scratched several of their heads, necks and chins, wondering how he'd get help if this went horribly wrong. Finally, emboldened by what he was seeing, he slowly reached out to one and gently touched its nose. He quickly withdrew his hand, then ever so gingerly tried again, leaving it a little longer this time. It felt like very soft, bumpy leather. From a finger touch to his whole hand to both hands, it wasn't long before Jeff and Angel were scratching the heads of several raptors who ran up for that treat.

"Unbelievable!" Jeff shook his head and then he started laughing. He laughed harder and harder. He couldn't help himself. Angel started laughing as well, prompted by Jeff's infectious laugh. They found a patch of grass in the middle of some ferns and sat down. It took a while to regain their composure. Once they stopped laughing, they sat there in silence, the raptors having run off, a couple of brachiosaurs and a giraffe lounged nearby.

"I think I needed that," Jeff said, wiping tears.

"You've been through a lot," Angel acknowledged. "Just dying is…well…quite an event, to say the least. Reliving your mortal life, seeing your mother again, meeting your ancestors and being reunited with your dogs; learning about a whole new world of spirits, and to top it off, petting a pack of raptors—any one of those is an amazing experience in and of itself. It's not unusual for new arrivals to feel overcome by emotions."

He paused for a long moment. Two large eagles and a Pteranodon passed together overhead. Jeffrey stared at them until they were out of sight, then looked at Angel, smiled and simply shook his head.

"You'll have limitless opportunities to explore Jurassicland and learn about everything here, so for now let's focus on your questions. I'll answer some now and then I have a surprise for you, so we'll get to the rest of them later. What's on your mind?"

A surprise? Jeff was intrigued, but sensed he had to wait to find out. He took a deep breath and was silent for a long moment.

"First, I have to say again how amazing all of this is. I feel like I'm dreaming, but I know I'm not. And you've been a great guide, if I can call you that. You've made it easy and comfortable, even fun!

"And what a beyond-beautiful world. It's all the best elements of Earth in one spot, but more glorious. Since I've been here, I've seen mountains, oceans, lakes, sand dunes, red rock, forests, this swamp, and more. I even spotted some snow where it looked like it was too warm to have any. Then all the different animals, including some I'd never seen, living together in peace. I could never have imagined this in my wildest dreams."

Angel had a big smile on his face, remembering what it was like to pass over and witness this stunning world. "Because everything on Earth was created spiritually first, unless it is something man-made, you'll find it here in the spirit world. Earth is a physical replica of everything that's here."

Jeff jumped in, "Yes, but even more amazing than all the physical things are the feelings I'm having. This might sound kind of dumb to say, but it feels like I'm actually breathing in peace and love. It's that tangible!"

"It's not dumb at all. Many share that same thought, even after acclimating to being here. I try to not take it for granted. Keep going. Share everything on your mind, so I can see the direction you're going, then we'll go back and explore as many topics as we can until it's time for your surprise."

"Okay, here it goes. I can't describe how wonderful it was to see my mom. I was relieved more than you'll ever know that she isn't suffering anymore."

Jeff had to pause to keep from getting emotional. He took another deep breath and continued.

"But please help me to understand *why*. Why would someone that wonderful have to suffer so much? If you only answer that one question, I'll be satisfied."

Angel nodded understandingly. "Noted. Continue."

"You said Nick would be okay. What's going to happen to him, and who were those guys in white—those paramedics I saw? Was I hallucinating or were they with you?"

Angel laughed. "You weren't hallucinating. I'll explain. Other questions?"

"Was it my time to die, or was that an accident? I thought I had a long life ahead of me, so this was a surprise, to say the least. And then, as we left Earth, how far did we travel? How far are we from Earth right now? Am I able to go back and visit, like my grandpa did when he watched my games? I'd like to see how Jake is doing. Plus, you and others have physically touched me. I can actually feel you, but I was floating above the boat on Earth, and they couldn't see or hear me, so I can't tell if I'm a ghost or something tangible."

Jeff was speaking very quickly now, anxious to get it all in.

"Where does this spirit world fit in and what's next? I mean, I don't want to sound disrespectful, but I thought I would have seen God by now. Did I mess things up or something?" That made Angel chuckle. "I know that's a long list, but that's what is on my mind."

"Those are all good questions," Angel replied. "And of course you messed up." He paused and seeing that Jeffrey looked surprised, continued, "We all do! But I know what you meant, and we'll get to that."

Jeff sighed a breath of relief. He didn't feel at all judged by Angel, yet it was nice to have his heavenly friend assure him that he was on the right track. He sat back against a smooth rock.

"That's good to hear. I'm ready to shut up now and listen."

He reached down and started rubbing Harley's head with one hand and Arnie's with the other.

"Consider the possibility you've been listening all along, here and on Earth," Angel responded, seeing an opportunity to teach a brief lesson. "We're always listening. The key to effective listening, however, is to be aware of when we're listening to our own thoughts, our own self-talk, or to the other person. My sense is that you've done a good job of giving me your full attention since we met. I do have the advantage, of course, of being a messenger from God," Angel added, chuckling. "Let's just say not many people ignore me when I come to pick them up!"

Jeffrey laughed at that observation, as Angel continued.

"I'm going to ask you to clear your mind as best you can. Just take a deep breath and be fully present."

Angel paused and did what he asked Jeff to do. He closed his eyes, took a few slow, deep breaths, then opened his eyes and went on.

"In addition to listening more effectively, quieting our minds helps get us in touch with our innate wisdom, as well as promptings from the Spirit. We would all benefit by doing it more often, more consistently. We go through life having a myriad of experiences, but rarely slow down enough to reflect on what they mean and what we can learn from them, even or more especially things we don't like, or that are uncomfortable or painful for us."

"I had to learn to quiet my mind, especially in sports," Jeff responded. "I think I got pretty good at it. You can't win games if you're distracted."

"It's good you had some experience with that. I think that in this setting…"

"I mean, where would I have been," Jeffrey interrupted, "as a football player, playing golf, even in my classes if I'd been distracted by other stuff?"

"A good point," Angel said calmly. "What I'm asking…"

Jeffrey jumped in, "My coach even told me that the more I could quiet my mind, the more I'd be in the zone and really excel. It's something I think I'm pretty good at."

"How do you think you're listening right now?" Angel inquired.

"I think I'm doing pretty well. I'm hearing everything you're saying."

"I told you I would mirror back thought habits as they surface, and you agreed to that approach. Are you still open to that?"

"Of course," Jeffrey replied, confused as to why this would be coming up now.

"This is the first time we've really engaged each other in a lengthy, meaningful conversation. I notice that you're very quick to respond to some of the things I've said. A couple of times, I didn't even finish my sentence, so it makes me wonder if you're *really* listening."

"The only reason I was quick to respond," Jeffrey quickly responded, "was because I heard what you said and agreed with it. What's wrong with that?"

Angel sat listening…reflecting.

"I really did catch your meaning," Jeff added. "I'll bet I could repeat back just about every word."

Angel took another deep breath. "This isn't about a behavior called listening. It's about your thinking, about quieting your mind. Imagine for a moment a well with water at the bottom. If I toss in some pebbles, I want to hear them hit the water. Right now, it feels like there's a piece of Plexiglas covering the top and the stones are just bouncing off. When you go quickly to what you know, you stop learning. You're not open to other insights or perhaps to seeing something you already know, but at a deeper level."

Jeffrey sat there with his brow furrowed, trying to make sense of what Angel was saying.

"There! That's the pause I was looking for. I can hear pebbles hitting the water."

Jeffrey nodded, connecting with the analogy. He wanted to say that he really got it but sensed that it was a good time to just stay quiet.

"We'll explore more of what might get in the way of your learning later on. Let's get back to your questions. As I said, I'm going to answer some now, some later. Others will unfold as you have more experiences in the spirit world. You'll need to be patient. Those answers will mean more when you're truly ready to receive them. Your first concern—to understand your mother's suffering—will take more experience here, as well as some things we'll view on Earth, but you'll get there. She will also have some of the most important insights into that question if you ask her."

Jeffrey quickly jumped in, "But what if…" He caught himself, shook his head and smiled, "Wow, that didn't last long. I guess I'm working on a new habit. Bear with me."

"Good catch," Angel said. "Let's go back to your drowning and start with Nick. You were worried he wouldn't be okay. It won't be easy for him at first, losing his best friend, as well as the guilt that can accompany being a survivor. But he's strong and as I said, he'll be fine."

"I'm glad to hear that," Jeffrey sighed. He felt Angel's assurance and trusted it.

"The paramedics, as you called them," Angel chuckled, "were two angels sent down to let Nick know it wasn't his time—that he had to return to his body. You could tell he didn't want to go back. Most don't. Not only did Nick want to stay with you, but he also wanted to stay, because he felt the peace and love most people experience crossing over."

Jeff agreed, "I tried to let our guides know not to revive me—that I was doing great—but they couldn't hear me. I never thought I'd say this, but I'm glad they failed."

Angel knowingly nodded and continued, "As far as the angels, they've been mistaken for many different things, including as you thought, paramedics. One of the funniest I heard was a guy who died stranded on a raft in the middle of the Pacific Ocean and thought that an ice cream vendor had come to help him! We're not thinking too clearly at that moment.

"The reason you can feel me, and everything here is because spirit is actually matter. Think of the tiniest possible particles. What we're made of at our core is more refined than anything on Earth, including the cells that made up our bodies. Spirit passes through anything physical on Earth, but spirits can touch each other, because we're made of the same stuff. That will enable you, answering another question, to visit Earth at different times. You'll be amongst human beings without being seen or heard. How are you doing so far?"

"It's fascinating. Keep going," was all Jeffrey could say. He knew there was so much to learn, yet he knew he could relax and soak in what he could.

"You'll remember that I welcomed you to Paradise. Paradise isn't heaven. It's a spirit world between mortality and final judgment, allowing God's children to continue to progress, ultimately to become more Christ-like. We need this period to grow, further develop our characters and help others do the same. There are literally billions who haven't yet even heard of Christ. Here we have the opportunity to share His beautiful gospel, so that everyone has the same opportunities."

Angel continued. "Let's talk about the distance to Earth. I don't know literally how far the spirit world is from Earth. You're likely thinking in terms of miles or perhaps light-years. In the spirit world, everything is connected by the portals we've been using, so it's more in terms of the distance of a thought. Once I think of and focus on a place I need to be, a portal opens that will transmit me there. You'll understand that better as you continue to experience it but know that we have immediate access to Earth whenever we desire or when a specific need arises. You've experienced this several times since your death—the tunnel that brought us here, your mom and other loved ones arriving to greet you, even your dogs jumping through light, and it's of course, what got us to Jurassicland," Angel smiled.

"I'm sure all that has created even more questions for you, but that's enough for now. That's a lot to digest. Let's get to your surprise. Some of your questions will be answered as we go to this very special meeting."

"Meeting? What meeting?"

Angel signaled for Jeff to follow him. "Several days have passed on Earth since your death. We're going to your funeral."

Chapter Five

As the two spirits came to the end of another portal, Jeff found himself standing in the sky over a town on Earth. His stomach turned when he saw how high they were. He was terrified of heights. Looking up while ascending after his death hadn't been a challenge. Looking down was different. Jeff reached over and grabbed Angel's arm to steady himself. After a few seconds, that didn't feel like enough support, so he latched on with his other hand as well. Had he not wanted to appear so scared, he would likely have bear-hugged his heavenly guide. It took everything he had not to.

"Relax," Angel assured him, gently prying one hand off his arm. Angel then sat down on…nothing…and motioned to Jeff to do the same.

Confused and frightened, Jeff gripped Angel even tighter with his right hand and started flailing his left arm, trying to keep his balance in the air. He looked down, confirming how high they were and started to feel dizzy. He panicked, waving both arms, and started sinking.

"I'm falling!" he yelled.

Angel stood. "Look at me," he said firmly. "Look at me!"

Jeffrey looked up at Angel. As soon as he did, he stopped descending. His body paused for a moment mid-air, then started to rise. He kept his eyes locked, afraid to look away for even a second.

"You're okay. Just quiet your mind and trust me," assured Angel.

Jeff continued to rise until he was again standing next to Angel. He reached out for Angel's hand, but it didn't come.

"Now slowly bend your legs and feel the air support you."

Pausing for a long moment, keeping his eyes on Angel, Jeff very slowly leaned back, bending his body, and felt a cushion of air start to support him. The lower he inched, the stronger the support became. In a moment, he was literally sitting in mid-air.

"Wow!" Jeff exclaimed with a shaky voice.

"Like walking on water," Angel smiled. He could tell Jeffrey was too distracted to get the reference. "Just continue to relax." He sat back down next to him.

"Rule number two in the spirit world. You bring the same personality into the world of spirits that you had on Earth." Angel paused. He could tell his student was still shaken by the experience. "Jeffrey, focus and listen. You're fine." He could see Jeff slowly relaxing.

"Many, if not most think they will be automatically changed to some sort of new creature when they die. That isn't the case. Death is simply a step forward in our eternal progression. What we make of it is up to us, but we continue the journey largely where we left off. We have the same basic strengths and weaknesses, the same tendencies and habits, many of the same fears and insecurities. Some of those leave right away, like the fear of dying of course. And some fears dissipate quickly once people experience the remarkable feeling of love in the spirit world. You clearly have the same fear of heights, though I think you'll overcome that rather quickly. You have other weaknesses to tackle, as well as traits to develop. It's all part of Father's plan for our eternal growth. More on that later. What do you see around you?"

Jeff was hesitant to look anywhere but at Angel, but he slowly broke his gaze and started to look around. Seeing once again how high they were, he quickly, instinctively reached out with his right hand and gripped Angel's left arm. Angel left it there. Jeffrey guessed that he was doing pretty well by sitting on an invisible chair above the Earth, so Angel was cutting him some slack.

As the two sat mid-air, Jeff looked up to see if the sky was overcast but was surprised to see there wasn't a cloud in the sky. He realized that Earth, even brightly lit by the midday sun, paled in comparison to the glory of Paradise. Everything looked dingy, even on a clear day. It took a moment from this angle to recognize, but Jeff realized they were hovering over where he lived…had lived…his entire life. This was his town. He spotted his home a few blocks away.

Looking straight down, Jeffrey saw they had come to rest directly over the church he had attended. People in Sunday dress, many in black, were entering the building. There was a hearse parked at the end of the sidewalk leading up to the main door. As he looked closer, he was surprised to see the roof of the chapel starting to open to his gaze. It became transparent and he could now see people sitting in the pews. Jeffrey looked over at Angel, pleased with this new aspect of his vision, then looked back down. As he did, he and Angel started slowly descending to where they had a better angle to view the proceedings.

Jeff continued to relax, fascinated with what he could see was about to happen. *Wow! My own funeral!* He'd never even considered this would be something he would see first-hand. There were two floral arrangements at the front of the chapel. The flowers looked bland compared to what he'd been seeing in the spirit world, but he realized that, in earthly terms, they were pretty bouquets. Some of his friends from school and work were sitting together toward the back. The rest were neighbors, some friends of his mom and a few cousins he recognized. He spotted Nick sitting next to his parents several rows from the front. He looked miserable, washed out, with dark circles around his eyes.

"There's Nick. He doesn't look good," Jeff said quietly.

Jeff then noticed his dad and Jake sitting next to each other on the front row. It took only seconds to see that dad had been drinking. He looked sad and deflated.

Serves him right for treating us the way he did, Jeff thought.

It was Jake though, who really got his attention. He looked dejected, sitting there quietly, slouched down in the pew a few feet away from his dad. Jeff wished he could assure him that he was not only okay, but extremely happy. And mom! He wanted to tell him that their sweet mother was completely fine.

Just then, Jeff spotted a coffin below the podium, topped with a spray of flowers, with a nice, framed photo of him on an easel nearby. He realized his dead body was there in the coffin, which gave him a start. He hadn't even thought about seeing himself at his funeral.

"Am I in there?" Jeff asked.

"Your body is," Angel clarified. "The *real* you is right here with me. Take a look inside. I think you'll find it interesting."

Jeff stared at his casket. It slowly became transparent. He could see himself lying on his back, eyes shut, hair neatly groomed, dressed in his dark blue suit, a white shirt and his favorite tie. He took a long, deep breath and soaked in what he was seeing.

It was remarkable. That had been him not long ago. Now it was an empty shell. He felt so much more energy, more life, more……..everything! Still in this moment of reflection, he felt a sense of gratitude for the earthly body that had served him so well.

Then something struck him. He realized that every part of his body was there – his skin, muscles, bones, nerves, arteries, organs – yet something was obviously missing. It was his spirit, what made him…him. He wondered why he hadn't noticed that when he'd lived on Earth. There was clearly something more than this body, and he was now experiencing it to the fullest in the spirit world.

Jeff glanced around the congregation taking it all in, and for the first time, instead of friends and family, he saw, really saw a group of spirits clothed in human bodies. He remembered something his pastor once said about us being spirits having a human experience. He didn't understand it at the time, but now it made a lot of sense.

He looked back and stared at himself a little longer in the coffin, then looked at Angel.

"You're right. It's amazing," Jeff said. "Not only is it not scary, but I'm feeling a lot of gratitude for my life."

"Many think they would be frightened seeing their own dead body," Angel responded, "but for most, it's a touching and fascinating experience. It looks like the service is about to begin."

Jeffrey and Angel positioned themselves to the right of the casket where they could see the speakers at the podium, angled so they could see the congregation, as well. They continued to sit mid-air. Pastor Bob rose to speak.

Just then, Jeff heard a rustling above and ahead of where they were sitting and noticed many flashes of light. There was another congregation forming, also sitting in rows, each slightly elevated behind the other. It looked as though they were sitting in stadium bleachers, but Jeff could see between them and determined they were all floating, along with him and Angel.

He recognized his deceased relatives, the ones he met when he arrived in the world of spirits. Instead of tears, they had expressions of joy. Jeff felt someone take his left hand. It was his mother sitting on his other side.

"Your special day on Earth," she smiled, "and for us as well. We're all here to celebrate your life." The two stood and embraced, then sat back down together.

For the next hour or so, Jeff got to enjoy this gathering in his honor. Though it was sad for those in the chapel, it was touching and uplifting to him. One close cousin and two of his friends spoke. Two neighborhood church members harmonized on one of his favorite songs. Jeff had once helped some friends organize a committee to help struggling students. One of the students they had assisted spoke. This was the most touching part of the service, hearing how this young man's life had been lifted through their efforts.

As the meeting drew to a close, Jeff's pastor asked if anyone else wanted to say anything in his honor. There was a long pause, then Nick stood and made his way to the podium. He stood there for a long time, not saying anything.

"Jeff was a great friend," he choked, then couldn't speak again for several moments. "He was always there for me. I let him down. It's my fault he died. I should have saved him," he said intensely. "I should have been the one to die. I'm so sorry!" Nick quickly left the podium and went back to sit with his parents. His mom put her arm around him, while Nick cried.

"That's not right!" Jeff exclaimed. "It wasn't Nick's fault." Turning to his mother, "Mom, it was an accident. Nick didn't do a thing!"

"I know that Jeffrey. We all do."

Jeff turned to Angel. "You've got to go over there and tell him. You've got to get through to him. I think he'll listen to you. It wasn't his fault!"

"He's not ready to hear that now," Angel said. And in the same calm, but steady voice that had earlier stopped Jeff from sinking added, "Trust me. The time will be right…"

"But he's really struggling right now. Why don't you just…"

"Jeff, listen to me. Timing is important. Please trust me until you get a better handle on how all this works. He's in good hands with his parents," Angel assured him.

Jeff slowly sat back, still frustrated. He wanted to somehow communicate with his friend, but knowing he had to have trust, took a long, deep breath, nodded and turned his focus back to the tribute, glancing Nick's way at times to see how he was doing.

The pastor pulled everything together at the end by delivering a beautiful sermon on Christ's resurrection, attesting to the hope we can all have of life after death. *I've heard that many times, but am now living it – literally living it*, Jeff thought to himself. There were closing comments; gratitude from the pastor for all who attended, and the service ended. The spirit world visitors smiled in his direction. Jeff felt a tremendous wave of love and appreciation from them, not only for the life he had lived, but for how pleased they were to have him with them. Then in a blink, they were gone.

In the chapel, six of Jeff's friends and cousins positioned themselves around his coffin as pallbearers, ready to take his remains to the hearse. The organist, a nice elderly woman who lived at the end of his block, played while the congregation stood in respect. Once the coffin was outside, everyone else filed out.

"That was a beautiful service," his mother remarked. "I remember when you and Jake sang together at mine. Yes, I was there," she said, seeing Jeffrey's surprised look. "I was so proud of the two of you. Jeffrey, I want to visit with you again soon, but I need to leave you now," said his mother. "We'll catch up."

Jeff wasn't sure why his mom had to go at this moment, but he hugged and kissed her goodbye. He was getting ready to ask Angel why she had to leave when he saw two of his football buddies approach his father. They were clearly hesitant to say anything.

"We're very sorry for your loss," one of them offered. "We went to school with your son. He was a good man."

"Well, he's dead now, isn't he?" Jeff's father coldly responded. "Going on that trip was a stupid thing to do." He turned and walked away.

Jake, who had been standing next to his father mumbled a quick, "Sorry guys. Thanks for coming," before walking quickly the other direction.

"Jerk!" Jeff exclaimed. "He couldn't even be nice at a time like this. I hate that man. I don't care if you are an angel. He's a mean, abusive drunk, and I don't want anything more to do with him. I hope Jake moves as far as possible away from him."

"Keep an eye on him, will you?" Angel asked.

"Of course. He's my little brother."

"No, keep watching your father."

Angel's tone was calm but firm. Jeff wanted to stay with Jake, but knew he had to let his brother go while he focused on his dad. He glanced over to make sure Jake was okay and saw he was leaning up against the black town car parked behind the hearse. He turned back and watched as his father staggered down the aisle. They both followed. Turning into the foyer, his dad ducked into the men's room and into a stall. Jeff guessed he was there to throw up, as his father sometimes did when he drank too much, but instead saw him sit on the toilet, fully clothed, put his head down and start to sob.

Jeff didn't know what to make of this. He just kept staring not knowing what to do or say. He heard the restroom door open, looked over and saw his pastor come in. His dad quickly stopped crying. Pastor Bob paused, then knocked quietly on the stall door.

"Brother Morris? It's Pastor McKinney. It's Robert. Are you alright?"

"Go away!" Jeffrey's father angrily responded. "I don't want to talk to anyone."

"That's fine," the Pastor tried to assure him. "You don't need to say anything. I'll leave you alone in a moment. I just want you to know that I'm here for you." He paused. "And that, most importantly, God is here for you."

Jeffrey could see both men on each side of the stall wall – his father sitting on the toilet with his head down, and Pastor Bob standing by the stall door with his head bowed. He appeared to be praying. There was a long silence.

Jeff's father finally spoke. "Don't tell me there's a God unless you mean someone or something that hates us and is delighting in our misery. No all-powerful, loving Being would have killed my wife, then taken my beautiful son. Get out!"

"I understand. I'll go. The funeral procession will be leaving for the gravesite in a few minutes. I'm sure you'll want to be there. Again," Robert said gently, "let me know if I can help in any way." He left the restroom.

Jeff was stunned. He couldn't remember his father saying a single positive thing to him or about him since his mother's death. Hearing him use "beautiful" to describe him was confusing, but Jeff quickly wrote it off to the alcohol and was now angry at how his dad was treating his Pastor, especially when he had come in to help. He watched as his dad slowly stood and made his way out of the restroom.

"Can we go now?" Jeffrey implored Angel. He wanted to get away from his father.

"Yes, we can go. There's more to the ceremony you'll want to see."

Jeffrey and Angel went up through the roof and over to the hearse, now loaded with his coffin. Jake was telling the funeral director they couldn't leave without his dad, but just then, Jeff's dad came out the side door and crawled into the limo.

"Guess we're okay to go," said Jake, and reluctantly climbed in next to his dad.

∞∞∞

The gravesite service was brief. Jake, his dad, a few friends, and a few cousins, as well as the pastor were there. Pastor Bob said a beautiful prayer, dedicating the spot as a final resting place for Jeffrey's body. He implored that those who visited this place would feel peace and God's love. Jeff had always liked Pastor Bob and was grateful for him planning such a beautiful day.

At "amen," the cemetery workers stepped up, placed the bouquet of flowers by the side of the grave, pressed a button, and the coffin carrying his body slowly and quietly descended into the ground. The pallbearers, one by one, unpinned their boutonnieres, dropped them onto the lid of the coffin, paused a moment in respect, then turned and walked away. The group dispersed, but several gathered close to where cars were parked and continued in quiet conversation. Jake and his dad were driven off in the limo, Jeff guessed to be taken to their home. He was torn. He wanted to stay close to Jake but didn't want to be near his dad. Angel distracted him from the decision.

"You'll like this." Angel beckoned Jeffrey to come near one of the groups that had remained. "These are the stories that weren't told at the podium."

Angel and Jeff enjoyed the next half-hour as friends and family told stories about him. One of Jeff's favorite comments came from one of his old teammates.

"Jeff and I played football back in the day. It was so funny. Here was this smallish, gentle guy who didn't have a mean bone in his body, but when he put on a helmet, he became this monster defensive back. He was half the size of the guys he'd hit, but they could barely get up! Then, to make matters worse, he'd reach down with that goofy smile of his and offer to help them up. I don't know if he realized it, but that rubbed it in even more." Everyone laughed together.

"Way to go, tough guy," Angel chided. Jeffrey wondered if spirits could blush.

Another nice comment came from a woman at his work.

"I knew Jeff from both work and school." Jeffrey was surprised. He didn't realize they'd gone to school together. *"He went out of his way to be nice to everyone."* Those in the circle nodded in agreement.

Angel wasn't done teasing. "Be careful you don't get a big head, or you'll never wear another helmet." Jeff laughed and shook his head.

The common theme as people visited was that Jeff was quiet and unassuming, the guy who some looked at almost as a little brother. Several times he and Angel laughed as funny memories were shared. Some details were exaggerated for the story's sake, but it was fun nonetheless, and what could Jeffrey really do? He just kept shaking his head, enjoying the moment.

At one point, his friend Charlotte tearfully shared how much Jeff had helped her when her sister had died. The fact that he understood her so well having lost his mother, had given her hope and consolation at a difficult time.

Once the impromptu gatherings had dispersed, Jeffrey turned to Angel and thanked him for this wonderful surprise.

Angel nodded. "I know the feeling from my own funeral. It's literally a once-in-a-lifetime experience." He paused. "I'm sure you noticed Nick wasn't at the gravesite."

"Yes, but I'm trusting you that he'll be okay."

"Because of free agency, I can't guarantee anything one hundred percent, but knowing what I know about Nick and about human nature, I'm sure he'll be fine."

"You mentioned your own funeral. Do you mean you lived on Earth, as well?" Jeffrey was surprised.

"I did. My life preceded yours by about forty Earth years."

"Why didn't you tell me? That seems really significant."

"It hadn't come up. I'm happy to share highlights at some point."

"I never imagined that angels might come from Earth. I guess I don't know what I thought. Maybe that angels have just always been angels. I'll need to get my head around that one. Is it time to go back to the spirit world?" Jeffrey inquired.

"No. First, I want you to see something for which most don't stick around. It's a personal preference. I like to sit by the grave, watch while they fill it with dirt and reflect on the life of the person who's crossed over. I did that with my own body, and it was a sweet moment. You'll be going forward quickly from this point on, so taking time in this setting to reflect is, I think a healthy thing to do."

Angel and Jeffrey walked over and sat by the open grave as a large backhoe pulled up and started filling the hole with dirt that had been covered by a green tarp, now lying nearby. At one point, the large shovel swung right through where they were sitting, making Jeffrey duck and throw up his arms to protect himself, while Angel sat there calmly. Once it had safely passed through them, they both chuckled.

"Yep, we still bring our personalities," Jeffrey admitted. "I'm not sure how you get used to that."

"Give it time," Angel responded.

As they sat there watching the large shovel fill the hole, Jeffrey thought back on his life. He'd had bad moments for sure, especially the death of his mother and his tough relationship with his dad. He'd also barely survived a nasty car accident that kept him laid up for months, but right now he was simply feeling appreciation for all the good he'd known. And what a beautiful spot this was – nicely groomed grass and tall trees. He looked around to soak in details of where his mortal body would rest.

Then Jeffrey spotted someone in the distance, standing half-hidden behind a tree – a young man who appeared to be looking right at him. The guy waved in his direction. Jeff looked over his shoulder and saw no one behind him. This person was waving to him. He then started walking his way.

It took Jeff a moment. "Craze?! Crazy Masey? Is that you?"

"You got it, bud. How's it hangin'?" Jeff stood and they gave each other a hug, loudly slapping each other on the back.

"Angel, this is…" Jeffrey paused. He'd called him Craze for so long that he couldn't remember his name.

"Marty. Marty Masey." He shook Angel's hand. "Friends call me Craze, at least they did when I was alive."

"I know Martin," Angel smiled warmly. "I'm aware of everyone who had a role in your life, Jeffrey. That was part of my preparation to mentor you. I'd like to give you time to get caught up. I'll find you when you're ready. Nice to see you, Martin."

Something about his leaving seemed a little mysterious to Jeff, just as his mother saying goodbye, but he was learning to trust Angel. He smiled, nodded and watched him disappear in a flash of light.

"Dude! It is so good to see you!" said Craze. "I heard you were coming but wanted to hang back while you did all the family stuff. Nice funeral, too, man. A lot more good things said about you than me when I bit it, but that's kind of how we each lived, right?"

"I guess," Jeff answered a little uncomfortably. "Am I supposed to call you Martin now?"

"Martin, Schmartin. Call me Craze or Crazy. Both work for me," he smiled. "Crazy Masey. Made me feel like I was part of the gang."

Martin Masey had attended college with Jeff for one school year. Well…for half a year until his climbing accident. He'd been free-style climbing – no ropes, no equipment – and had fallen from a cliff to his death. Those who got to know him were sad, but no one was surprised because that's exactly why Marty had been nicknamed Crazy – Craze for short. He'd take risks no one else would come close to. He and Jeff hadn't been that close of friends but had done enough things together with a larger group that it was a fun surprise to see him.

"Guess they let anyone in the spirit world, huh?" Crazy teased.

"Do you mean me or you, Craze?" Jeff joked back. It felt a little odd calling him that as a spirit, but it seemed to make Marty happy.

"You, of course!" Craze laughed. "Actually, it's great to see you, man. As I said, I heard you were coming and have been waiting for a chance to catch up, but I didn't want to interrupt the reunion. Going to your own funeral is a pretty cool thing, isn't it?"

"Beyond words," Jeff nodded.

Craze couldn't hold back his excitement. Under his breath, he exclaimed, "Dude, when you're ready, I have the most amazing thing in the universe to show you. Can you come now?"

Jeffrey glanced around. The crowd had dispersed, Angel was gone, and the crew was done burying his body.

"I can't think of any reason why not. What's it all about?"

"Just focus on me and you'll keep up. We're heading to a very cool world."

And on that cryptic note, he was gone.

Cool world? What could he mean by that? Maybe he was thinking of Jurassicland and doesn't know I've already seen it, Jeff thought.

But Craze was gone, and Jeff had to catch up. He thought of Marty, stepped forward, and disappeared from Earth.

Chapter Six

Jeffrey could tell from the pleasant brightness surrounding him that he was back in the spirit world. He and Craze were standing in a large, open field which though simple, was beautiful, just like everything else he had seen since he arrived, even more so having just been on Earth.

"Okay dude," Craze could hardly contain himself. "I need your permission to do this."

"Permission to do what?" Jeff asked cautiously. Everything he remembered about Crazy Masey indicated that trusting him wasn't the smartest thing to do.

"I'm not going to tell you. It's a surprise. You'll know soon enough. And hey," Craze said mischievously, "it's not like you're going to die or anything."

Oddly enough, that's a good point, Jeff thought. *What could he really do to me here?* He nodded. "Okay, I'll take a chance."

"Not just okay. I need you to say out loud that I have your permission."

Jeff scowled and sighed, "Okay, you have my permission." He quickly added, "but if you do anything…"

He didn't finish the sentence.

In an instant, Jeffrey Morris was no longer himself. He was now David Whittingham. As the successful founder of a major online retailer, David had the time and money to explore the world, drive fast cars, go on safaris, scale mountains, and today would free fall on his own for the first time. No more tandem diving. He'd earned the right to parachute without assistance.

What David didn't know was that his oldest son, David II, impatient to claim his inheritance, had promised someone a large sum of money to stage an accident. The son knew his dad would insist on packing his own chute, in spite of everyone's objections. That would provide the perfect alibi for his death. Dad's well-known ego would lead to his unsuspected demise.

Jeffrey/David stood near the door of the plane. Once the signal came, he leapt straight out, arched his back and spread his arms and legs. He shouted with joy at the exhilaration. Flying through the air, he allowed himself to soak it all in – the landscape below, blue sky all around and beautiful white clouds on the horizon. It was perfect. After several more seconds, the Dytter altimeter in his helmet sounded a warning tone. David glanced at the altimeter on his wrist and confirmed that it was still in the green portion but nearing yellow.

He reached across his chest and pulled firmly on the rip cord. Nothing happened. He waited a moment for the assuring tug of his chute catching the air, hoping against logic that somehow, he just hadn't felt the release, but still nothing.

As a leader and adventurer, David had been in tough situations before and knew how to keep his head. He reached across and pulled the cord on his safety chute. Still nothing! Perhaps ten long seconds passed, and the ground was coming up quickly. He panicked. A deep, powerful fear overcame him. He started clawing at his back, trying desperately to free the chute.

The victim hit the ground with tremendous force. Though it only lasted a fraction of a second, the pain that every nerve in his body felt at once was profound.

Suddenly, there was a bright flash of light, followed by a feeling of joy more intense than the pain he'd felt seconds earlier. He was filled with pure, euphoric relief. As the burst of light and the accompanying feeling slowly decreased, he saw Craze standing there, grinning from ear to ear. They were back in the field.

"Well, what do you think?" Craze excitedly asked, "How was it?! I know the death itself was pretty quick compared to others we'll do, but the panic preceding it really added to the moment, right?"

Jeffrey was unable to respond, trying to catch his breath. "What the hell was that?!" he finally yelled, trembling from the experience.

Crazy laughed. "Heaven, my friend. Hell's an entirely different place."

"No, seriously. What was that?!"

"I call it the ultimate death rush." To emphasize the point, Craze shifted his voice to a tone that reminded Jeff of a radio commercial where a deep voice excitedly announces that weekend's stock car races. *"Nothing like it in the universe,"* he gushed. "How was it?!"

Jeff stood there with his mouth open, shaking his head, incredulous at what he'd just experienced. He sat on the ground to gather himself. "How did you put me in that guy's body? I mean, I became him. I was David Whittingham. In an instant, I had a past, a family, a job, I even knew where I'd travelled in my…in his life. I had no memory of my true self at that moment. How did you do that?"

"I actually don't know, dude," Marty responded. "I experienced this powerful rush right after I died on Earth, falling off that cliff, and wondered if I could replicate it. I've been playing around with the portals ever since and just kind of fell into it…no pun intended. I've been experimenting and found a way to recreate different deaths to experience that euphoria each time."

Jeffrey was still trembling. He wasn't sure if he should thank his friend for the joy and relief he felt or see if it was possible for one spirit to smack another for torturing him that way. His death had been horrifying, but the ecstasy of passing over not only made the pain disappear but filled him with a pleasure that was much greater in contrast to the physical and emotional pain.

In spite of the happy ending, something about it was troubling. Jeff couldn't put his finger on it, but as amazing as it felt, it didn't seem right. Before he could question any further, Craze asked if he was ready for another one.

"Are you serious?!"

"Hey, did it feel amazing, or what? I have another awesome scenario for you, this one even more intense."

"I'm not ready for that, at least not right away."

"Oh, don't be a wimp. Don't you trust me?" Craze implored.

Jeff had always hated disappointing people. He was torn – he didn't want to do this again, at least not right now, but he also didn't want to hurt Craze's feelings.

"Of course, I trust you," Jeffrey said reluctantly.

"You know what to do."

"Alright, I give you permission…"

Jeff instantly became Harold Anderson, a college student who worked evenings in a restaurant at a local ski resort near Denver, Colorado. Hal, as his family and friends called him, was driving home. He had just finished his nightly routine cleaning the kitchen, making sure everything was ready for the breakfast staff in the morning. They'd had a very busy night, with a large group coming in right before closing. He noticed on the dashboard that it was almost 2 a.m., much later than when he'd usually head to his apartment. It had started snowing that afternoon, so the winding canyon road was quite slippery, in spite of the road crew's best efforts. Hal was ready to relax in the safety and warmth of his home. He remembered he had homework to do in the morning for one of his classes, but for now, was focused intently on the road.

As he rounded a sharp bend, his car, which should have turned right, hit some ice and kept going straight, veering into the other lane. Hal's heart skipped. If any cars were coming up the canyon, he'd slam right into them. He hit the brakes hard, feeling the grinding of the automatic braking system as it quickly kicked in to help keep control. He tried frantically to turn the wheel to get the car to respond, but it only turned at a slight angle. The car and driver crossed the opposing lane and toppled sideways over the side of the high mountain road.

Everything was happening quickly. The car flipped and rolled down a steep embankment. As it finally rested at the bottom of the ravine, Hal was hanging upside down, freezing water from the creek filling the top of his small car. He knew he had to get out quickly, but as he grappled to unlatch his belt, the gas tank exploded. Though it was only a matter of seconds, it seemed like an eternity before Harold Anderson succumbed to the fire ... and his mortal death.

A bright light quickly followed, an indescribable euphoria, then Jeff found himself back in the meadow.

"How was that?!" Craze asked excitedly.

Jeff was shaking – a mix of shock from the experience, but also clearly feeling the rush and relief that came from dying. He sat down again, his head bowed, taking deep breaths, his trembling spirit slowly recovering. He finally looked up and asked, "How does that happen? You must have some idea."

"No clue, dude," Craze laughed. I know I have to keep doing more and more intense stuff to get the same feeling. I've been cooked by cannibals, ravaged by a pack of wolves and slowly crushed by a steam roller. I was recently in a medieval torture chamber and you wouldn't believe what I was able to endure. What a rush!

"Turns out it's not only those who die the most painful deaths who feel the greatest release. It's also those who die surrounded by intense hatred or persecution. I've let myself be a martyr burned at the stake a few times and it was awesome! That's why my friend, for your dying pleasure, I chose a really painful one – the accident, the fear of drowning, broken bones, then the fire. It should have given you quite a sensation."

Craze paused and smiled, "Dude, I have one more for you, and this one's even better than the first two."

Jeff winced. This was more than he could take.

"I promise this is the last one for now. Do this one, and I'll leave you alone for a while. But seriously man, isn't this the best?! There are a million ways to die and you've only experienced two of them, three if you count your own."

Jeffrey took a deep breath and stood. "I've got to tell you, Marty, I don't feel good about it. It's nothing against you. I feel like we're taking advantage of something we shouldn't be messing with, even making light of it. Yes, the rush of dying is amazing, but it just doesn't feel right."

At that moment, Angel appeared. His light seemed brighter than when Jeff had last seen him. Craze quickly stepped behind Jeffrey, getting out from between him and his angelic mentor.

"Hello Jeffrey and Martin. Nice to see you." They both nodded their greeting. Then Angel gently inquired, "Jeffrey, how are you feeling right now?"

Jeff had several emotions running through him at once. He'd felt peace, for the most part, since being released from Earth, but now there was confusion and turmoil. He felt strongly that it was wrong to do this, yet he didn't want to hurt his friend's feelings, and the deaths he'd experienced had admittedly given him a remarkable rush. He could see why Craze would find this so…well…addicting.

That's when it hit him. There was a difference between the light and joy he'd felt when he met Angel and what he'd experienced with Marty as he died in different ways. The former feelings had increased and deepened with each encounter with a loved one, with thoughts of gratitude or from warm memories of his life. The rush he felt the times he died with Craze was momentary – a bright flash of light, but one that diminished quickly. It even felt that he eventually lost light or at least that deep feeling of peace with each deathly adventure.

Angel was smiling. Jeff didn't have to express himself verbally for Angel to know what he was thinking, partly because Angel could see he was once again increasing in light.

Craze could see what was happening to his friend. "Killjoy," he muttered, knowing he'd just lost another companion in death. "I'm outta here. I'm going to go be eaten by a shark." And with that, Crazy Mazy disappeared.

"I guess I messed up," Jeff said, feeling a little embarrassed.

"Not at all. Let's call it a learning experience," replied Angel, "I encouraged you to go with Martin, suspecting this is what would happen. You're not the first, and certainly won't be the last to try this. As I told you before, these are all growth opportunities to gain knowledge and light, just as your mortal experiences were on Earth. Everything in our lives has the potential to be a lesson – some great, some small – but all potentially for our progression. What do you think you learned from this?"

"The rush I felt each time I died," Jeff answered, "was intense, but it didn't last very long, except for my own drowning, if you include that. A moment ago, I was thinking this might be what drug addicts experience on Earth – a momentary high, but one that dissipates quickly. Craze, I mean Marty, even said he had to keep doing more and more intense deaths to get his high."

Angel nodded. "Remember, we bring the same personality with us. Those prone to addictions on Earth have the opportunity and challenge to overcome different forms of addictions here. They're surrounded by love as hopefully they are on Earth, which helps a great deal, but the conviction and determination still has to come from within. It's difficult, but achievable. Tell me about your choice to die a second time with Marty. You seemed reluctant, but went ahead, even though you'd done it once."

"I'm embarrassed to say I didn't want to hurt his feelings. Deep down, I knew I shouldn't do it. It just didn't feel right, but I've been a pleaser most of my life."

"Was there a time on Earth when you were afraid to hurt someone's feelings and wound up paying a significant price for it?" Angel inquired.

The answer came quickly to Jeff, having reviewed his life recently. He suspected that might be one of the reasons people experience their whole life after passing over, so that fresh memories could be used for learning, though this one he knew intimately.

"My car accident," he conceded.

"And what happened there?" Angel knew, but also knew it would be important for Jeffrey to talk it through, to gain his own insight.

"The guy who was driving was high and didn't even have his license. I didn't want to get in the car, but everyone was asking me to go and I didn't want to say no. The guy even said, 'What? You don't trust my driving?' I answered that of course I did, and got in.

"Looking back, the right answer was, 'No, you idiot! I don't trust your driving,' and I should have walked away. Some of my friends might have even followed me, but we all chickened out together. We're lucky no one was killed, but it caused months and months of pain and rehab for me and for Nick, because of my desire to get along."

"This seems to be something worth exploring," Angel encouraged, "and I have a suggestion as you do. Don't beat yourself up. Just stay curious as to what you do well, and what you could do better, including how you need to think differently to make a change. Guilt or regret tend to keep us stuck. Humility and openness to improve on the other hand, demonstrate a growth mindset. If we hurt someone or mess up along the way, having genuine remorse and demonstrating a commitment to change is a very healthy way to grow and progress. God calls it repentance."

"Makes sense, though I still wish I'd handled it differently. It's hard not to get down on myself." He paused. "What was that portal Marty used to make me die different ways?"

"Do you remember seeing holodecks that were used in science fiction shows – the ones where they experience virtual reality all around them?"

"Yes, I loved that idea as a boy. Was that one of those?"

"Sort of, but much more advanced. We call it simply our Experience Portal. Though it's not exact – no one but God knows perfectly what you think and how you feel, it approximates the memories, the background, the situation at that time, and even the feelings closely enough and as you experienced, powerfully enough, to teach some remarkable lessons. It is a great instrument for learning empathy. Like most tools though, it can also be misused."

"Like Marty repeatedly dying?" Jeff asked.

"Yes, and there are other ways. Let's say someone had always dreamt of having fame and fortune. He or she might use this portal to briefly become a rock star, singing the final big number in a concert with thousands of screaming fans. That can be fun a few times, and I've even tried it. But there are those who keep doing it over and over and over. They're not happy being themselves, so they're stuck – avoiding the opportunity to learn to love themselves and to find and develop their God-given talents. Once they learn to use it wisely to progress, earthly sensations, like fame and adulation, don't matter and they really start to grow."

"This is fascinating," replied Jeffrey. "The possibilities seem endless."

"They are, and with no time constraints, there's so much we can learn. One other caution for you though. These portals, if used too often, can also desensitize you. Marty keeps dying again and again. He's acknowledged he needs to keep dying more painfully to feel the blessings that accompany death, but he's also missing the negative aspects – that death adversely impacts so many, including loved ones left behind. It's like watching repeated deaths in movies, without seeing or experiencing the real consequences of each person dying."

"Then how does it develop empathy? I guess to use it sparingly?"

"Yes, and thoughtfully. Let me have you experience a powerful scenario. May I send you somewhere?"

Jeff was reluctant. Even though he completely trusted Angel, he was still a little shaky from his last two deaths. Angel assured him that it wouldn't involve dying.

"Then yes, I give you permission."

In a flash, Jeff became a mother of a young family in a small village in a third-world country. Her day-to-day, even moment-to-moment concerns centered first on survival – how to feed, clothe and protect her family; such basics as how to provide clean water each day, to say nothing of how to raise and eventually educate her loved ones, so they would have a better future – all of the daily worries that weighed her down.

And with that simple, brief insight, he was back.

This time, Jeffrey was silent for quite a while, but not from the shock of pain and euphoria of death. Angel waited patiently, knowing what was happening to his friend.

Jeff finally spoke. His voice was subdued. "I've understood intellectually that there are people struggling in the world. I've just obviously never felt it the way they do. You're right – that was so powerful. If I had truly comprehended that on Earth, I would have tried to do so much more."

"That only took you a moment, but it's just one of many examples that help us connect with and understand each other in more meaningful ways here in the spirit world. It's something of which I hope you'll avail yourself going forward."

"Count on it," Jeffrey replied.

"On a lighter note, you can't imagine how many wives bring their husbands here to experience childbirth. Now *there's* a humbling experience!"

They both laughed a little nervously.

"What's going to happen to Marty?" asked Jeff.

"He'll be stuck in his progress until he's truly committed to give this up. In fact, it will become boring to him because he'll run out of things to experience to get that higher high. I believe he'll make it, but he'll have to dig deep." Angel paused. "On a related note, what if anything, might this have taught you about death and God's love?"

Jeffrey paused, reflecting on his experiences.

"I think God makes death, the moment of passing over, pleasant because of His love for us and because it's the one thing that all of His children have to go through. Maybe those who suffer most or the longest, or who die facing extreme hatred or persecution, maybe even heroes that die are especially rewarded."

Angel wasn't surprised at Jeffrey's insightful answer. He was a good student and was ready for his next level of learning.

"You're ready to move forward. First, why don't you go be with your mother, do some more catching up, then I'll pick you up again to continue your tutoring."

Jeffrey liked that idea, nodded, and both were off in a flash.

Chapter Seven

"The last time we held class, it was in 'Jurassicland,'" Angel said smiling, still amused by Jeffrey's label. Where would you like to hold class this time? We can return to the dinosaurs, or you can choose someplace different," he offered.

"Well, what have you got?"

"Picture your ideal setting. It doesn't have to be somewhere you've visited – just a place you've imagined or really wanted to visit – and describe it to me."

Jeffrey said, "That's easy. It's like where I died…. I mean the first time," he quickly added. "There are high mountains, a beautiful river or lake, and some wildlife. It's that kind of place."

In the blink of an eye, Angel and Jeffrey were standing in what he had just described, but with everything lit from within, so even more glorious. The towering mountains were jagged and multi-colored. A nearby lake was shimmering, with ducks and swans paddling in small groups. The crystal-clear water revealed scores of multi-colored fish, each with its own heavenly light. A river emptied into the other side of the lake, and as Jeffrey's eyes followed it farther back, he could see a majestic waterfall in the distance. The two were surrounded by brightly shining wildflowers of all types, their light scent filling the air. And all around were animals grazing on the grass, some glancing over to acknowledge their guests. It was idyllic.

"Nice choice," Angel nodded, looking around. They both just stood there in silence and soaked it in, then finally sat down on the shimmering grass.

"Jeffrey, you asked earlier why you were allowed to pass over, and Nick was sent back. In simplest terms, it was your time to come here, and it wasn't his. God has a specific plan for each of us, and we're experiencing that plan whether we're on Earth or in the spirit world."

He continued, "In a way we can't yet understand, Father is intimately connected with *all* of His children. Just as not even the smallest bird dies without His knowing it, He is fully aware of each and every one of His sons and daughters on Earth and here in the spirit world. God continually supports and guides us in ways that will best further our growth and development while we experience life in its different forms.

"At the same time, God is what you might call the ultimate Team Player. He wants us to become more aware of each other's needs and do our best to help each other, especially through difficult challenges. Both efforts are going on at the same time – Father's support and ours. In fact, He often answers prayers through others close to the person in need, as well as through spirits on this side. Make sense so far?"

"I think so," replied Jeffrey. "It makes me think of what you told me earlier that part of the purpose of our existence is to become more Christ-like, especially in serving others. If God did everything for us, I don't think we would grow very much."

"Right. It's like a smart parent," Angel added. "If moms and dads did everything for their children and didn't allow them to be challenged, it would stunt their development. In this case our Father, the ultimate, perfect Parent, communicates eternal truths through His prophets, leaving us our agency as to whether we follow them to our benefit or we don't to our detriment. When we do, we grow in ways that He knows are most beneficial for us in the long run.

"At the same time that God is speaking through his chosen servants, there is a group of volunteer spirits that do their best to influence and inspire our brothers and sisters on Earth. I'm one of them. We're asking you to be part of that important effort. What do you think?"

"I'm honored. I really am, but I don't feel worthy of it. I certainly don't deserve it," stated Jeffrey.

"You're right, you don't. But then, none of us do!" exclaimed Angel. "This isn't about somehow deserving it or not or being better or worse than others. We just do our best to serve in spite of our weaknesses, while we're still growing ourselves. Others who feel unworthy or incapable will also be given the opportunity. There are actually millions of us who have raised our hands to serve this way."

"But, when people on Earth can't see or hear us, how do we influence them? And how would I even know what to tell them, if I could?" asked Jeffrey.

"The 'how' is primarily through feelings and impressions, just as Father does. He provides guidance for those who will listen through His prophets and their written words, but personal inspiration and direction for our lives is more subtle. He speaks through the Spirit to our hearts. That's similar to how we communicate as volunteers. We talk to people. The recommendations we make are less than a whisper to those on Earth. Some hear or feel and heed them, many do not.

"As far as the 'what,' we'll start with four basic principles called *angel traits*, which, though simple, are profound in their impact. Angel traits are ways of being, time tested over many eons, which help us all live and function at our best more often and more consistently. We'll begin with those four traits and expand from there."

"What do you mean ways of being?" Jeffrey asked.

"These are more than simple actions. They're ways of thinking or showing up in life that are as powerful for us in the spirit world as they are for our sisters and brothers on Earth, regardless of one's religion, belief or even lack thereof. If more people lived by these principles, the world would be a better, happier and more productive place.

"In addition to the four, there is a fifth principle I'll eventually share with you – different in its nature – that once truly understood, will have the greatest impact of all. I'll be teaching that to you in real-time after we explore the foundational four."

Jeffrey wanted to know the fifth principle now, but knew he'd have to wait. He suspected and thought it ironic that it might be patience, which made him chuckle.

"Let's jump right in," Angel beckoned. "You won't learn these angel traits in any particular order of importance. Each is most significant for the person that needs that principle at that time. I want you to observe something. Let's stand up."

As he stood, Jeffrey was surprised when what looked like a small house formed all around them. He and Angel appeared to be on Earth, standing in someone's living room. There was a flower-patterned sofa directly ahead of them, positioned in front of a curtained window. There were family pictures on a wall, a small table with a lamp by the sofa and a coffee table directly in front of them that had mail, magazines and toys strewn about. What caught Jeff's attention was a man, directly in front of them, sitting on the sofa, staring right at them. Jeff froze and stared back. He didn't recognize the man. Sitting next to him was a little girl who looked to be about six years old. She was facing her dad, one leg dangling down the front of the sofa, her other folded up underneath her.

Jeff spoke very quietly, "Is this real? Can they see us?"

"Yes, it's real," Angel responded, "but you can talk normally. This image is being broadcast in real-time from Earth, but they can't see or hear us. It's like a 3-D movie in which we can walk around and observe without being seen ourselves. Kind of cool, huh? Makes for a great classroom," he nudged Jeffrey to make the point, who rolled his eyes and smiled.

"We'll start with what is unfortunately, a very typical challenge. Watch this father and daughter and tell me what you see."

Jeffrey watched as the little girl tried to get her dad's attention. "Daddy, can you come play with me?"

No answer. The little girl's father was still staring at Angel and Jeffrey. Jeff turned and saw that the dad was watching a football game on television right behind them. He was looking right through them, which seemed funny.

The girl paused, then tried something different. "Daddy, I'm hungry."

"In a minute! I'm watching a game." The father was clearly irritated by the interruption.

The girl waited a bit, then ventured, "Daddy, will you read me a story?"

"I told you I'm watching a game! Now leave me alone!" he answered gruffly.

The little girl got up and walked out of the room. They followed her down a short hall into an adjoining bedroom and watched as she sat on the floor and started playing with one of her dolls. The father didn't move, still glued to his TV.

"What do you see?" asked Angel.

"I see a cute little girl with a dad who is a jerk," Jeff responded.

"Try to be a little more diagnostic," Angel encouraged.

"I see a little girl trying to get her dad's attention, and a dad who is too absorbed in his football game to do anything else."

"Good. Now what do you think the impact is on the little girl?"

"She looked sad and disappointed at first but seems okay now." Jeffrey was looking closely at the little girl, now playing happily with two dolls she was holding face-to-face in conversation with each other. "I guess kids bounce back pretty quickly."

"Do you think it might have a long-term impact?"

Jeffrey paused. "Doubtful after just one time, but I guess if it happened over and over, she might grow up feeling disconnected from her dad, maybe even resentful."

"You're right. Now here's a more difficult question. What do you think the impact is on the father?"

Jeffrey followed Angel as he walked through the wall back into the living room. '*I wonder if I'll ever get used to doing that*,' he thought. They watched the dad for a few minutes.

"He doesn't seem phased by it," Jeffrey observed. "Maybe that's just the way he is or has always been."

"Okay, hold that thought while we switch to another scene."

In an instant, Jeffrey and Angel found themselves in a different home, this time in the kitchen. There was a different man than they'd last seen, sitting at the table typing on a laptop. A little girl galloped in through the backdoor yelling, "Daddy! Daddy! Come play on the trampoline with me."

"Hey sweetie," he responded, "I'm right in the middle of an important project for work. And anyway, you know I'm a klutz on the trampoline. Maybe we can play something else later."

"Okay," said the little girl. She turned and walked slowly out the back door. Jeffrey noticed her head was down.

"Another jerk," Jeffrey said, upset with the dad.

"Keep watching," Angel said, nodding toward the father.

Jeffrey noticed the dad wasn't looking at his computer anymore. His eyes followed his daughter as she walked out of the room. He stared at the empty doorway. He then smiled, hit a couple of keys to save his work, closed the laptop, and walked out into the backyard. The heavenly observers followed. The little girl was already jumping on the trampoline.

"Hey, you!" the dad yelled with a smile. "What are you doing jumping without me?"

Before she could answer, the dad ran to the edge of the trampoline, clumsily climbed up and started jumping. The little girl squealed with delight. In a flash she was showing off, effortlessly doing front flips, while the dad just jumped up and down on one end of the trampoline.

"You're really good at this," he said to the girl's clear pleasure. "The most I can do is 'sitsies' and 'kneesies,' and not even those very well."

"Show me," said the little girl.

"Hmmm…you might want to have an ambulance standing by!" joked the dad.

He came to the center of the mat, jumped up and down many times, trying to get some height and clearly trying to get up his nerve. The dad looked so serious that both Angel and Jeffrey started laughing.

Then, he bounced up high in the air and stuck his legs out to land on his behind. He threw his legs up so hard that he hit the surface leaning far back and flipped over backwards, landing on his stomach, doing a face plant on the mat. The little girl gasped, but her father rolled over on his back and laughed heartily at the sky. His daughter took three bouncy steps over and fell across his torso, making him grunt. They both just lay there, laughing together.

"I told you I wasn't very good at this," said the exhausted dad, wiping tears of laughter from his face. "Where's that ambulance I asked for?"

"I think they'd be laughing too hard to pick you up!" said the clever little girl, which made them both laugh again.

"How about I just watch you for a while?" asked the dad. "You're really good at this," he repeated.

Dad crawled over to the corner of the tramp, pulled himself onto the metal frame and sat, focused on his daughter. She was clearly pleased to demonstrate her skills and kept glancing over to make sure her dad was watching. The father's eyes never left her.

"What did you observe?" asked Angel.

"I saw a dad being a dad," Jeffrey answered, touched by the moment.

"We call this angel trait, *'Be Present.'* It's about bringing all of who we are to the moment. This whole experience will only last about twenty minutes, but it will be much richer, more meaningful and memorable for both of them. Then the father will go back and get his work done in time for the deadline, and the little girl will be fine doing something else. Being present doesn't often take a lot of time, but it magnifies the impact of almost everything we do. Let's go back to when he said that he couldn't play," Angel suggested.

In an instant they were back in the kitchen, the scene reset to where they had started.

"I guess it shouldn't surprise me that you have instant replay," Jeffrey shook his head.

"With some enhancements," Angel responded. He reached over and touched Jeffrey's temple. Jeffrey felt a warm sensation.

"What was that? What did you do?" Jeffrey inquired.

"Watch this scene again and tell me what you see."

As the little girl ran in, Jeffrey could now see that she was emanating light. He could actually see the excitement she was bringing into the room. As the scene unfolded, the father told her he was doing some work, and said that they might do something later. At that moment, the light around the daughter seemed to dim a little. She turned and walked out of the room.

"Did I see what I think I saw? Did that light around her get dimmer? What was that, anyway?"

Angel nodded. "Yes, it decreased. Keep watching."

The dad had turned back to his laptop, but noticed his daughter was walking out with her head down. Then Jeffrey noticed something he'd missed the first time around. He'd been looking at the little girl and missed Angel whispering something to the dad.

"Be present," Angel quietly said.

As the dad watched his little girl, Jeffrey saw two things happen at once. The father rolled his eyes and shook his head, indicating he knew he'd missed an opportunity. At that same moment, a flash of light surged from his body.

"That flash of light indicated that he received an insight."

Jeffrey nodded, somewhat incredulously. "You mean each time we have an insight, we…we have a flash of light?"

"That's right," Angel responded. It doesn't last more than an instant. Mortals can't see it on Earth, but the more of those we have in life, and the more we act on those impressions, the more we grow in our overall capacity for light and love. Now what do you notice?"

The father was jumping on the tramp and he and his daughter were laughing together. Both had a constant light shining from within.

"Wow, it's beautiful," Jeffrey remarked. "I can feel it from here."

"These are some of my favorite experiences, played out in countless ways across the world. It's why I volunteer to do this. It might be a playful scene like this one, someone comforting someone who's sick, a teacher listening intently to a student, two people really connecting in a conversation. All of those are simple moments of focus, of being present, and of growing in light. Now, let's go back to the first example."

In an instant, they were back in the first living room, replaying the moment the little girl had walked out. Jeffrey watched as Angel did the same thing, whispering to the dad, *"Be present."*

How did I miss that twice? Jeffrey wondered.

This time the father didn't respond, keeping his eyes focused on the television. Jeffrey noticed that both his and his daughter's auras diminished a bit.

Angel added commentary as they watched. "This moment in and of itself, though unpleasant, won't be critical. We all have moments like this. But as we continue to miss those opportunities, the diminished light grows ever dimmer and can have a lasting impact. The way to reverse it of course, is to start having more positive moments, which we can do at any time in our lives. You'll see this play out when we review some of those moments in your life."

"We're going to look at my life?" Jeffrey asked a little uneasily. He suspected there might be plenty of examples of not being present with others.

"We'll view your life for a couple of reasons. First, who better to learn from than yourself, from your own experiences? You'll know whether or not you were being present, how you felt at that moment, what was going on in your thoughts and the impact on you and the other person or task."

"Task? I thought this was about people."

"Being present is being focused in the moment, whether it's with a person or the task at hand," Angel clarified. "We've learned over many generations that what isn't effective is to multi-task – to do it all at once – for example, working on a laptop, while listening with one ear and nodding to someone, while worrying about something else you could or should be doing. You'll see examples of that when we revisit your life portal. This is an opportunity to bring the best of who we are to the moment.

"The second reason we'll use your portal is that we're not watching people to judge them. When we see and acknowledge our own frailties, we can view them in others with empathy. This increases the chance they will feel and hear our impressions when we make suggestions. Think of your own life. When someone judged you and wanted you to change, how open were you to their criticism?"

Jeffrey didn't even have to answer that one. He nodded understandingly, now feeling bad he'd called the first father a jerk.

Angel continued, "The suggestions we make to people come from complete non-judgment. We're sincerely interested in their well-being and they unconsciously sense that from us. It doesn't guarantee a positive response, as you saw with the first dad, but it increases their chance of hearing and acting on it.

"The interesting thing about being present as influencers," Angel added, "is that the more in the moment we are, the better we'll hear and feel inspiration ourselves as to what we should whisper. Being present is a foundational principle that enables other principles and helps us better serve humankind. Come with me."

The two then revisited Jeffrey's life portal, pausing at key moments to observe how he had done with being present. Angel encouraged Jeff to start with the times he had done it well. He noticed that he lived very much in the present as a child, which Angel said was typical for most. As he watched himself getting older, he was pleased to see many moments when he was really focused on the other person, group of people or the task at hand. He saw when he had wonderful discussions with his mom, brother and friends, some moments brief, others extended. The light around them while they were being present with each other had a richness and wonderful glow to it. Jeff wondered, had he known this back then, if he might have somehow even felt that light.

Jeffrey noticed he'd been present quite naturally when playing sports. If he was in his head, distracted by thoughts of how he was doing, he typically didn't play well. When he was focused and present, he was more 'in the zone.' While up to bat in a baseball game for example, as he quieted his mind, he remembered that the ball actually looked larger and slower, even though it was coming at him at such a high speed. The power of focus, of being fully present, was remarkable in many ways.

Jeffrey also witnessed many times when he wasn't being present. It was interesting to reflect on the thoughts that pulled him out of those moments, whether it was worrying about the future or dwelling on the past, wishing he had been doing something else or judging another person.

Jeff noticed that his ego often pulled him out of the moment and connecting with others. While doing a presentation at work, he missed the nuances of the group and misunderstood their questions, because he was worrying about appearing smart or clever. Being present made him a better listener, being distracted didn't. Most of what he observed were simple instances, one-on-one, where he either chose to be present or was clearly distracted. It surprised him how noticeable it was, but then he remembered that he could tell when someone with whom he was speaking was really there, so why wouldn't they with him?

Some of the nuances of being present were very interesting. In one instance, during a high school football game, he recovered a fumble and scored a winning touchdown. Some cute girls came up to him the next day in school and congratulated him. He beamed and said it was nothing, though his countenance indicated otherwise. He failed to mention that his buddy Anton, standing right next to him, had made the hit that caused the fumble and then threw a key block that made the touchdown possible. It was subtle, but Jeff could see that Anton looked disappointed when he walked away. Jeff wanted to kick himself. He prided himself on being a good team player but had been distracted by his own ego and missed what was going on with his friend. He was confident he would have said something if he hadn't been so caught up in his own press clippings and making it all about him.

"Remember, be careful not to beat yourself up. This isn't about whether you, or anyone we're watching, is a good person," Angel prompted. "Just stay curious and learn from each example. We're all children of God – His divine creation – and we can always improve. It's that simple. We'll be making suggestions to our brothers and sisters as to how they can build on the goodness they have and live happier, more fulfilling lives, part of which is living more fully in the present."

Jeffrey nodded, appreciative of the support he felt from his angelic friend.

"Now comes the best part of what we do. Let's go inspire some lives," Angel said excitedly. "We go to Earth and look for people who are distracted. We won't have to look far. Then we tell them to be present. Some will hear it and some won't. It's a step at a time, a prompting at a time and when it works, it's gratifying to see the results.

"By the way, I know you well enough to know you'll want to see Jake and Nick when we go down there. They're doing okay. Nick's still struggling with the guilt, so he's extremely busy minded right now. His family is the best, most direct support. At the right time, you'll be able to support him, as well as your brother."

Angel seemed to have read his mind. Jeffrey knew he should trust his angelic friend and be present with him on this adventure.

"Lead the way!" Jeff exclaimed, and they stepped into a nearby portal.

Chapter Eight

"What a remarkable experience!" Jeffrey exclaimed as they returned from Earth. As Angel predicted, they had seen numerous examples of people not being present. Because of the sheer numbers, they focused on those for whom it would seem to have the greatest impact and, in a few cases, possibly saved lives.

The two weren't really surprised when they saw it but noted how many drivers were texting behind the wheel. Not all of the distracted drivers put down their phones at the counsel to *be present*, but they hoped they at least diverted some danger for those that did.

In a hospital, a nurse came into a patient's room busily recording vitals from a machine by the bed. Angel asked what Jeffrey noticed.

"She isn't being present."

"Actually, she's being very present with the task at hand, but overlooking the patient in the room altogether. She has a good caring heart. It's why she became a nurse. I suspect she'll react well to the suggestion. Why don't you go ahead this time?"

Jeffrey stepped up, leaned in by the nurse's ear and said, *"Be present with your patient."*

The nurse looked up and saw the patient, an elderly woman, watching her. "How are you doing, darlin'?" the nurse inquired.

"I wish I knew what was going on," she responded in a timid voice. "No one has told me what's happened since my surgery."

The nurse stepped over and placed her hand on the patient's hand. "The doctor will be here soon to explain everything. Your vitals are strong, and I understand that everything went very well. I'll come back in after he speaks with you to make sure you have everything you need. Anything else I can do for you?"

The patient seemed to relax and drifted off to sleep. The nurse was smiling and glowing as she left the room.

Several times they saw people arguing. They'd encourage everyone to take a breath and listen to understand, to be a little slower to respond – to be more present with each other, instead of with their anxious thoughts or need to be right. A few times expressions of anger seemed to lessen as they sought to better understand the other person's perspective. Sometimes it was simply to come at the challenge or opportunity fresh another day. Overall, those that seemed to respond to their gentle promptings got better results.

As Angel's student, Jeff realized quickly that being present was more than just listening, which was his initial impression. There were many layers to it. In one case, the two aided someone getting ready for an important job interview. Jeff could see that the young man, newly married with a young baby, had prepared hard for the discussion, but was sweating profusely as he was clearly doubting his ability. *"Be present,"* Angel encouraged, and added, *"You've got this. Be interested in the person interviewing you. Let go of what you've prepared – it'll be there when you need it. Quiet your mind, trust yourself, be present and you'll do great."*

They saw the young man close his eyes and take a deep breath, slowly letting it out and relaxing a bit. The interview seemed to go well. The young man engaged the interviewer nicely by being fully present and not caught up in his own worries.

Shortly after that, they spotted another distracted driver speeding toward a school zone. They quickly alerted him to *be present* and to literally slow down while he was figuratively doing so. Fortunately, he acted on the prompting. He'd clearly been thinking about something other than his driving.

Many they observed were similar to the father-daughter scenarios they'd watched earlier but were adult couples, one usually busy-minded and the other trying to get the other's attention. After a nudge from their invisible visitors, those who chose to be more present had a richer conversation and noticeably glowed as a result.

In one touching moment, both he and Angel noticed a young woman on her knees pleading in prayer for help. As they listened, they could tell she was struggling with work, finances and lost love. She was sobbing as she prayed. Angel whispered for her to *be present* – to listen to the promptings and comfort Father would send her. It seemed to calm her a bit.

After other varied opportunities and simple, but touching moments, they returned to the spirit world.

∞∞∞

"I see why you were excited to do that. Not everyone listened to us, but those that did seemed to access peace, understanding and clarity. It's a powerful principle."

"It's one of my favorites," Angel shared. "A simple concept that creates greater happiness and fulfillment. If that's all we taught, countless lives would be influenced for the better, including our own, but there's more. First, before we jump into the next topic, let's take a break and have some fun."

Fun in the spirit world? Jeff thought to himself. Angel's invitation was intriguing. *More dinosaurs perhaps?* He pictured himself riding a triceratops, gripping the bony plates on top of its head as reins to guide it around the swamp.

"I know you've grown up loving music. I have a special challenge for you. They stepped into a portal and landed in an expansive area filled with huge cumulus clouds, billowing as far as the eye could see. There, oddly situated in the middle of nowhere, sat a harp, a chair and a music stand.

"Your next assignment is to sit on this cloud and learn to play this harp. It's required of all our volunteers. You've never played one, right?"

Jeffrey shook his head, his brow deeply furrowed. No, he'd never played a harp. He'd never come close to wanting to. Was Angel serious? He had no idea how to respond.

Angel continued excitedly, "This is a talking harp. It will teach you how to play itself. Remember there are no time limitations here, Jeffrey. Just sit down, start strumming and in what will amount to only ten or twenty Earth-years, you'll be playing like a pro. Come get me when you're ready for your first recital."

Jeff remained speechless. This was a terrible turn of events. Not only was it so cliché to have him sitting on a cloud playing a harp, but to think that Angel somehow thought this would be fun was mind-boggling.

Angel paused, a completely serious look on his face as he waited for Jeffrey's response…and then he started laughing. At that moment, Jeff's mother stepped through a nearby portal.

"That's my boy you're having fun with," his mom said, both playfully and sternly.

"I know, I know," Angel responded. "This was one I couldn't resist. You should have seen the look on your face. That was one of the funniest I've seen."

"Practical jokes in the spirit world? Really?" responded Jeff, now laughing with Angel. His mother just smiled, shaking her head.

"You should know there are no talking harps here…or anywhere!" Angel was still laughing. "I made that up just for you."

"I'm honored," Jeff chided, rolling his eyes. He had to admit that, in spite of how silly and really unfunny Angel's joke was, just that he'd attempted it and that there could be a sense of humor in Paradise pleased him. He wondered what appropriate ways there were in the world of spirits to get back at Angel.

"Now that your mom is here, we are actually going to a musical event. This is serious, no more jokes and something I promise you'll love. After being so good natured, you've earned something special."

Jeffrey could tell Angel meant it this time and was intrigued. Together, the three of them stepped into a nearby portal.

∞∞∞

As they exited, Jeffrey saw a multitude of spirits gathered together, by far the most he'd seen since he arrived. Below them, Jeffrey saw a town on what appeared to be Earth. He noted a specific view had opened, so he and the other spirits could see into the top of a home. It had the appearance of an old cottage, two levels, with a thatched roof. Jeff could see a man sitting at a desk with a quill pen in hand, parchment paper before him with an ink well by the side, the desk lit by a candle. The pages had blank treble and bass clefs used to compose music. Other pages were scattered around the room, filled with a detailed composition.

"To appreciate this moment, you need to know that Father has created countless worlds throughout the universe," Angel explained. "The planet you are seeing isn't Earth. It's *an* earth, but not *our* Earth. This earth and its people are a few hundred Earth-years behind ours."

"What? Another earth?!" This was quite a revelation to Jeffrey. He and Angel were looking at a populated planet that wasn't their own! He didn't know what to say, given the significance of what he'd just been told.

"Keep watching," encouraged Angel.

As Jeffrey looked around to soak in the scene, he noticed hundreds of spirits who had taken out instruments to form what appeared to be an extremely large orchestra. A dignified looking man who had been sitting with his back to them stood and moved in front, facing the musicians with baton in hand. He was elevated, so everyone could see him.

"That's George Frederic Handel," said Angel quietly.

"*The* Handel? The one who composed 'The Messiah?'" Jeff asked incredulously.

"Yes, though technically, George didn't compose it, at least not from scratch. He received it by revelation and refined it through his experience and through inspiration. The original composer, Fritz Jung, is there on the front row," Angel said, pointing to a man sitting close to the orchestra. "Fritz composed the original 'Messiah' thousands of years earlier on an earth that preceded ours. Those spirits sitting on either side of him were chosen to bring it to their planets when the time was right. 'The Messiah' has been shared with at least eight other planets since its creation. Each time it's revealed, the last composer to receive it, in this case, Handel, from our world, has the honor of conducting it, so it can be received on yet another world. In this case, the one we're watching below."

"I can hardly believe what I'm hearing," said Jeffrey.

"They're about to start. Quiet your mind, *be present*, and we'll discuss it more when they're done. I'm sure you have a lot of questions." Angel responded.

Jeff watched as the composer in the house below leaned his head back and closed his eyes with quill pen in hand. The light immediately around him grew brighter.

"Based on his light, he's reflecting, opening himself up to inspiration," Angel said quietly. "Now enjoy."

Watching the scene below carefully, and seeing that the new composer was ready, Handel lifted his arms, held that pose for a moment, waved both arms up, then in a down beat as the orchestra started playing "The Hallelujah Chorus." This was Jeff's favorite piece. He had sung it in choir. On cue, hundreds if not thousands of choir members, literally singing angels, filled in the verses. The music poured into Jeffrey's soul like a powerful wave. As the piece progressed, tears flowed freely. He noticed he wasn't alone. Everyone in sight seemed overwhelmed by the heavenly chorus.

"Hallelujah! Hallelujah!" the choir's voices filled the heavens. Jeff looked down and saw the composer writing furiously. He remembered his choir director saying something about Handel perceiving the heavens being opened as he wrote the Messiah. *Was this how it happened for Handel*, he wondered?

As the music reached a crescendo with "King of Kings and Lord of Lords," Jeff felt himself rising, floating with the music. Every fiber of his soul seemed filled by each note. He felt the same from everyone around him, as though the music was a wave of light and sound and emotion that permeated and connected them all as it resounded throughout the heavens.

When the last note faded away… all sat in silence. Handel with his head bowed, everyone in tears, the composer below still furiously recording his thoughts. The earth scene gradually closed. It took a while, but the spirits in attendance slowly rose, not a sound being made and disappeared into flashes of light. Everyone had clearly been lifted with joy and celebration. Jeffrey guessed correctly that they would gather again soon when the receptive composer was ready for more.

∞∞∞

The three moved through a portal to Jeff's mother's home. Even after their arrival, they didn't say anything for a while, the effects of the powerful music still resonating through their souls. Angel finally broke the silence.

"Well, what do you think?" he inquired, already knowing how Jeff would answer.

"I can't describe it," Jeffrey quietly responded. "I hope you both felt what I did." They nodded. "So, the Hallelujah Chorus wasn't just meant for our earth?"

"That would be rather limiting, wouldn't it?" asked Angel. "Who among God's vast creations wouldn't you want to have it? Fritz Jung created it by inspiration. He was encouraged after he passed over to share it with someone on a different world, someone who was designated and blessed to develop that particular talent. And so, it has been passed on, as one of Father's anthems to His Son. Each composer puts a slightly different spin on it, since they each perceive it a little differently, but it's basically the same. Handel was chosen and blessed to bring it to our world.

"All of God's children have gifts and talents," he continued. "Some are used more publicly than others, like Handel's, but all are ultimately meant to be shared in service for others and for the development of the soul." He paused. "What else did you learn from this?"

"I've always believed that music is a powerful force and inspiration. I still believe that, but it pales in comparison to listening to it here. I can't even describe it. It's a complete soul-filling experience, head-to-foot, inside and out.

"One odd thought struck me as we were leaving, that we were the 'outsiders' looking at another planet, kind of like space aliens to them, yet we obviously don't have the appearance of aliens, or at least how they're depicted in the movies. No elongated bald heads, no antennae, no extra eyes. I guess it's true that there is indeed life on other planets – lots of it – which is astounding, but we as God's children, all look basically the same. That was something I wouldn't have expected."

"Interesting observation. The truth probably wouldn't sell a lot of movie tickets," Angel chuckled. "Jeffrey, how would you describe the feelings that are bubbling up for you right now?"

Jeffrey bowed his head and shook it gently from side to side. "I'm feeling very small and humbled by the scope of all of this. To think of other worlds, the expanse of God's creations. My thinking and perspective have been so limited up to now. On the other hand, to know that God knows when a sparrow falls to the ground, that somehow He knows me – that He knows all of us personally…by name…how do I even fathom that? It fills me with a sense of profound gratitude."

"Perfect," Angel smiled, "because that's our next angel trait."

Chapter Nine

"The first angel trait, Jeffrey, is to *be present* – to bring all of who we are to the moment," Angel picked up where they had left off. "We'll never do it perfectly, but when we catch ourselves and come back into the moment, we get better results, have richer and deeper relationships and have more fulfilled lives, whether on Earth or here in the spirit world.

"To introduce the next principle, we're going to return to the spot where we landed after I picked you up from Earth – the place where you and your mother reunited. You didn't know it at the time, but it's a special chamber that's customized just for you. You'll be able to go there to reflect any time and can share it with others when you like."

All Jeffrey could remember of that initial setting was a large, empty, bright space, so the notion that it was customized for him was confusing. Still, he'd been surprised before in this fascinating world.

"Sounds interesting," he responded. "I'm ready."

"I'll see you soon," his mother said. "It will be fun to see what you come up with."

Jeffrey wasn't sure what that meant, but again, he pushed himself to remain patient and curious.

As they stepped out of a portal, Jeffrey recognized the completely empty, bright space, which he could now see was a large sphere. The walls looked like a bright, shimmering movie screen, curving around on itself to form a globe. Nothing had changed. It was still an empty room – the "customized" room Angel had promised him. He thought back on the harp and smelled another prank in the making.

"Love what you've done with the place, Angel. You really shouldn't have gone to all the effort," Jeff said, prodding his friend.

Jeffrey's glibness didn't faze Angel. He smiled. "Have a seat." He bent his legs and a portion of the spotless floor rose and formed a comfortable chair, catching him mid-crouch.

"That was cool," Jeffrey exclaimed. He paused a moment, smiled warily at his friend and slowly sat down, on guard for whatever trick lay in store. His customized chair quickly caught and nestled him, as well.

Angel leaned toward Jeff, "Bring to mind something for which you are grateful."

"What do you mean? Anything?"

"Yes, just tell me something that you really appreciate."

"Okay. My mom," Jeffrey offered.

At that moment a large, three-dimensional picture of his mother appeared on the screen in front of them. Jeff immediately noticed that it wasn't just three-dimensional. It exuded energy. He could see and practically feel the love and warmth in her eyes and smile.

"That's the most beautiful picture of her I've ever seen," Jeff exclaimed. "It looks like she's right here in person."

"Name something else," Angel said.

"Um, my brother, Jake."

A handsome picture of his brother appeared next to his mom's. As with her image, Jeffrey could see and even feel his brother's good-hearted nature, his love of life, his core energy.

"Wow! I see what's happening. I think I've got it from here." Jeff directed the screen, "Harley and Arnie." He paused. "Nick." He paused again and smiled, "Angel."

As he called out those names, beautiful, practically living pictures of each appeared on the screen.

"I'm glad these rooms make me look better than I actually do," Angel laughed. "Thanks for the honor. Try something inanimate."

"Nature," Jeffrey ventured, "like the place we had our second meeting."

A familiar scene appeared with mountains, a lake, trees, wildlife, and a cascading waterfall. The ripples on the lake shimmered, appearing like actual water. They could even smell pines in the distance.

"Amazing!"

Jeffrey continued to list those things for which he was grateful, the walls filling with glowing images. Because his thoughts were creating them, the pictures represented what was most meaningful to him. When he said "freedom," for example, a multi-faceted image appeared that had a flag, some soldiers, someone speaking at a rally, a clip of him voting, and his church – all symbolic of the freedoms he had enjoyed on Earth. When he said "music," one of his favorite songs started playing in the background.

"This is remarkable. Has anyone ever run out of space?" Jeffrey inquired.

"You can't. The room will grow as your list does, as your gratitude does. Technically, you could access a portal to see all of these in person, one by one. But being able to come here to reflect, to see them together can create wonderful moments of inspiration. Because the room is connected to your feelings and thoughts, those things for which you are most grateful at that moment will stand out for you. You can also 'play them' as a sort of movie in any order or grouping you wish. You might just say, 'play family,' and various pictures of your family will be highlighted.

"*Be Present* is our first angel trait. **Be Grateful** is the second. Gratitude is one of the simplest, yet most powerful mindsets we can develop. It instils in us humility and draws us closer to God than just about any other trait, especially when we acknowledge His hand in all His creations and blessings. This time, as we explore this trait, we'll start with your own life. As we do, continue to focus on things for which you are grateful."

They stepped into Jeff's portal and reviewed key moments of his life. He discovered that the spirit world had automatically been added to his history – his reunion with his mother and loved ones, Jurassicland, his funeral, the uncomfortable adventure with Martin, the inspiration and power of 'The Messiah,' and others since he'd arrived. The two wound up back in Jeffrey's gratitude room.

"How are you feeling right now?" Angel inquired, once they were seated, the walls covered with new lively images that reflected Jeffrey's appreciation.

"That's a leading question, since I know we're exploring gratitude. What's different is that, instead of coming out with so many different high and low emotions, as I did the first time, I viewed my life through a gratitude lens, which changed a lot of what I felt. As you'd expect, I'm feeling profoundly appreciative for the many blessings I've received throughout my life, so many that I didn't recognize at the time."

"And yet, you faced difficulties," Angel responded. "Some were extreme. Consider the prolonged suffering, then death of your mother, your father's alcoholism and abuse, the injuries you sustained in your car accident and other challenging moments. What do you make of that? Why aren't you feeling down having relived those moments, as well?"

"I guess seeing it all at once puts it into perspective. There certainly were things in my life for which I'm not grateful. Though now looking back, I can see how I grew through those experiences."

Angel smiled at that insight as Jeff continued.

"But at those difficult moments, I wasn't feeling grateful at all. I was miserable, even depressed. At times it seemed there was no end in sight, like when I was recovering from my accident or with my mom's sickness."

"You had every right to feel miserable," added Angel. "Sadness, mourning, even suffering is all part of the human condition. This isn't about wearing rose-colored glasses. It's about keeping things in perspective. It's acknowledging when we're able, even at the most difficult times, that there are always things for which we can *be grateful*. And when things are going well, it's important to remember the Source of our blessings and express that gratitude to Father. That can give us strength when things get hard, as they always do. Personally, I try to remember to express gratitude at the start of every prayer, no matter what I'm facing."

"Angels pray?" asked Jeffrey.

"Of course, we do!" Angel exclaimed. "We need guidance from Father as much as anyone. I kneel down frequently, sometimes in my gratitude room, and I'm always carrying a prayer in my heart."

"What do you mean by a prayer in your heart?"

"Just what it sounds like. It's an expression to Father that is unspoken, but that I'm certain He hears. On our last mission to Earth, when we saw that woman crying on her knees, pleading for help; I didn't kneel down next to her to formally pray, though I could have and sometimes do. I said in my heart, *'Father, this woman is really suffering. Please hear and answer her prayer.'*

"Or sometimes when I see or experience something beautiful, like the concert we just attended," Angel continued, "I'll say in my heart three simple words, *'Thank you, Father.'* I'm confident Father hears those simple prayers, as much as He hears and answers our verbal or more formal prayers."

"You said you've knelt down by some who are praying and joined them. Do you think there were angels praying by my side when I was struggling during my mother's illness and death?"

"I know there were," Angel answered gently. "Your mother was one of them after she passed over, as well as other loved ones you've met. I was there, too."

Jeffrey was touched realizing he hadn't been alone, even though he'd felt that way. *Thank you, Father, for that support,* Jeffrey said in his heart. Immediately he sensed that this simple message was heard.

"Given the importance of this principle," Jeffrey was curious, "what could I do to develop more gratitude in my life? And what would I suggest to others on Earth – simply to *be grateful?*"

"There is a two-part answer to your question. One is actions we can take, the other is deeper – it's about our mindset. As far as things we can do, there are many simple steps we could all take to practice more gratitude. Many of them are intuitive. Let's brainstorm them together.

"We can begin by reflecting on and journaling daily those things for which we are grateful. Sometimes the list will be long and come quickly, other times more slowly, depending on our circumstance in the moment. But the very act of slowing down to reflect on those things for which we are thankful and writing them down can have a positive impact. I once observed a man living with chronic pain who kept such a journal. He couldn't always muster up thanks for the things around him, but I recall in one instance, he simply wrote that he was grateful he'd had less pain that day. It seemed to lift him in that moment."

"That's really touching," Jeffrey replied.

"Acknowledging blessings, like the ability to read or write, to be wearing clean clothes or having access to pure water and healthy food, depending on where we are in the world are things we likely take for granted and for which we could be more grateful," added Angel. "Yet, we can't get into the comparison game. That leads to pride on one hand or coveting on the other. If I get to a point of being grateful for what I have in a proud way, instead of in humility and most importantly, don't willingly share those things with others, I'm on the wrong track."

Angel continued, "I remember a time in my mortal life when I was feeling down for no real reason and couldn't shake the feeling. I switched on the news and saw the results of a natural disaster that moments before had wiped out literally tens of thousands of lives. I remember thinking, *what in the world do I have to complain about?*' I started praying for those who had been impacted, which took me out of my own darkness. A little perspective goes a long way."

"You alluded to one I'd add to the list," Jeff said. "It's serving others. I know I could always do better at that, but it's hard to feel down when I get 'outside' myself and focus more on the needs of others."

"That's a great one and one that Father always encourages. I mentioned before that He often answers prayers through others, because it has the benefit of both people being blessed and lifted. I once watched parents agonize over a daughter who was off track with her life. They'd kept praying that their relationship with their daughter would improve – that they would be able to help her. The answer didn't come through them however, but through a teacher who connected with the girl and helped inspire her to turn things around. Things are still rough between the girl and her parents, but they are extremely grateful their prayers were answered in an unexpected way, through an unexpected person. Four people were blessed in that instance."

Angel went on, "You mentioning your mother's death reminds me of when I lost my parents. They weren't young when they died, as your mother was. They'd lived long, full lives. My dad was my best friend and my mother an amazing woman, so when they died within months of each other, I was filled with grief. Yet, there eventually came a time when I started to make a conscious choice that involved gratitude. When I started feeling down, usually on an anniversary of something I'd shared with them, I'd consciously choose to think about what a blessing it was to have them as my parents and to have those memories. I can't count the times in which sadness turned to gratitude and even 'thank you, Father' moments that lifted my spirit."

Jeffrey nodded and continued their brainstorming, "How about writing a note of thanks to someone, or doing something nice to thank them, without them even knowing it was you?"

"Related to that is the principle of paying it forward," Angel chipped in. "Passing along a blessing we've received to someone who wasn't involved in the first place. These are all good ideas, Jeffrey, and of course, there are others. It's a great question worth continually exploring.

"I mentioned there's a deeper answer to your question. We've enumerated ways to practice gratitude, all of which have the potential to lift our spirits and those of others. As we reflect often on things for which we are thankful, it becomes a *thought habit*, which we discussed earlier. You'll start to notice more often things around you that are life's little miracles, as well as things you can sincerely appreciate in others.

"My parents had such a mindset. One day when I was a teenager, my dad and I were working in the garden we had in our backyard. We'd been at it for some time and were resting, leaning on our shovels, when my father bent down and gently touched a flower. He pointed out the intricacies, the color, the scent of this tiny, beautiful plant. I still remember him saying, *'Imagine sticking a seed in dirt and having that come out. Even more remarkable, having a human cell join with another to create a human being. Don't tell me there isn't a God.'"*

Angel continued, "Mom and dad would often point out a sunset, a garden, a child, and other miracles around us. I'd roll my eyes and say, 'yeah, yeah…' but over time, they instilled in me a sense of gratitude. Looking back, I realize we didn't have much materially, but I didn't realize it because my parents sincerely and consistently lived in gratitude. It's also a spiritual gift for which we can pray, not only thanking Father for blessings in our lives, but asking Him to inspire in us a stronger sense of gratitude. That's a prayer I believe He particularly loves answering.

"At an even deeper level, we can feel gratitude even when it doesn't seem we have blessings to count. Start to notice your brothers and sisters on Earth who have almost nothing yet live in peaceful contentment. And for those who are struggling, as we all do at times, peace can be found through the Comforter, as well as faith in blessings that lie ahead, like being reunited with your mother. That's the hope Christ gives us. It doesn't mean we're happy that we're struggling, but there's an inner peace we can have as we draw closer to the Savior and do His will. That kind of joy isn't dependent on things around us but grows through our relationship with Him. For that, we can be eternally thankful."

"How are you feeling right now as we reflect on gratitude?" Angel inquired.

Jeffrey paused. "It's a warm, calm, pure feeling," he responded. "I'm in a good place."

"As am I. Right where we should be for our next adventure. We could talk about this more, but let's go spread some gratitude on Earth. Look for opportunities to suggest, *'be grateful,'* and watch what it does when people listen. Gratitude also ties in nicely with being present, which you should continue to pass along when you see the opportunity. It's hard to be out of the moment when we're fully in gratitude mode. By the way," he said, leading the way to their opening transport, "I'm grateful I get to experience this with you, my friend."

"As am I," replied Jeffrey with a smile.

Chapter Ten

Angel and his parents, and Jeffrey and his mom were visiting Jeff's mother's home. When the two returned from messaging *gratitude* on Earth, they thought it would be nice to introduce their parents to each other, as well as in that same spirit, thank them for everything they had done in their lives.

It had been a fun visit. Jeffrey learned about Angel's life on Earth and how in some ways it paralleled his own – his interest in sports and music, for example. He suspected and had it confirmed that those similarities were likely why he'd been chosen as his mentor. The biggest surprise was that Angel's name was William. His friends had called him Will. Angel…rather, Will suggested that Jeffrey call him that going forward.

"It was fine as you got to know me, but since several of our volunteers are also called Angel, it will avoid confusion," William clarified.

"Will it is," said Jeffrey.

Jeff enjoyed learning about Will's parents and their history and especially more about his mother's. It was interesting how similar his struggles were to hers, even though they were from different generations. The manifestation of the challenges was different, with growth of the internet, social media, key inventions, societal shifts and more, but the personal burdens they each faced through fears, insecurities, physical pain and other struggles helped Jeffrey see they had much more in common than he ever realized.

"Considering your extended family's interest in your life," his mother observed, "hopefully you see that you were surrounded by loved ones who understood and who could support you remarkably well, even with those generational differences."

"Then why was life so difficult?" Jeffrey earnestly asked. "Mom, it just about killed me seeing you suffer that way."

She took his hand as she answered. "I've reflected on that many times. Father wants us to grow in ways that we never imagined and to understand that we are stronger than we ever thought. Think back to when you were lifting weights for football. How much would you have grown if you'd kept the weights the same every time?"

"Not much," Jeff acknowledged.

"My analogy falls short, because life's challenges are of course, much, much harder and more prolonged than lifting weights, but the principle is the same," his mother continued. "We grow through adversity, sometimes tremendous adversity. I remember at times getting to the end of my rope, knowing I had nothing more to give, and yet at that moment, another challenge was thrown my way. It felt like the universe was piling on just when I couldn't handle any more. I now know those are the times I grew the most."

"So does God create challenges for us, even tragedy at times, or are they accidents – consequences of nature and a world He set in motion?" Jeff inquired.

"That's something that has been debated for centuries, Jeffrey. But I think it's the wrong question. It's something we won't understand until this is all wrapped up and everything is revealed. In the meantime, the more important question is whether God is there for us through all of our challenges, regardless of who or what caused them. I've found that He is.

"Looking back, I realize God knew better than I what I could ultimately handle. He was building…or more correctly…He was helping me discover and develop my internal, dig-deep strength. And yet, ironically as much as He wanted me to get in touch with that strength, He also wanted me to learn that

I could only do it with His help. My core strength was a gift from Him and at the same time, He blessed me beyond my own means to handle whatever came my way. Make sense?"

"Sort of," Jeffrey slowly responded, "but it's easier now that I'm here and can see you're not suffering anymore. It was devastating when I was in the thick of it."

"I know," Jeffrey's mother conceded, "but that comfort we gain here is available to us on Earth as we pray for strength and understanding. Father finds ways to speak peace to our hearts even in the most difficult of circumstances, if we're willing to listen. We don't avoid the pain – that's part of our growth – but the assurance that Father is there for us can come to all. We are after all, His children. Loving parents don't keep their child from struggling, since they want their child to grow, but they provide comfort, love and encouragement when needed. And though we as parents are far from it, He's perfect at knowing exactly how and when to do that.

"There's one other aspect of your suffering you'll find to be a blessing. I understand this will be part of your upcoming training, but if William doesn't mind…" she looked at him.

"Please," he nodded back.

"I think I'm catching on as how to best maximize your learning, my son, as well as my own," she smiled. "Let me just open this portal."

Jeff's mother stood and waved her hand in a broad motion. The walls of her living room disappeared and the five found themselves standing in a church on Earth. To their left was a tiny coffin. As they looked closer, they could see a little girl in a white dress lying inside the small box. She had the sweetest face and appeared to be asleep. Sitting on top of the coffin in spirit form, was the same little girl in the same white dress, her legs draped over the side. She was looking very lovingly toward her parents who were receiving condolences as part of her viewing.

There were people lined up to pay respects to the grieving parents. The mother was sobbing, the father clearly trying to be stoic. Two spirits, an older man and woman stood behind the couple, one with his hand around the father's back, the female spirit with her head lovingly on the mother's shoulder. Jeffrey guessed correctly they were deceased grandparents of the girl.

"Come close," Jeff's mother beckoned.

As they listened in, it was clear that people were struggling with what to say to the devastated parents. They'd share a special memory of the little girl, something they treasured about her, often concluding by saying that the parents would remain in their thoughts and prayers. One man said he'd just lost his best friend, his dog of fifteen years and so he knew how they felt. He suddenly sensed it wasn't the best comparison and tried awkwardly to clarify.

"Not that your daughter was a pet. I mean, I'm not trying to say…"

"I know what you mean," the mother said tenderly, taking both his hands. "They're like members of the family. I'm so sorry for your loss."

"That's all I was trying to say," said the man, grateful he'd been understood. "I'm so sorry for your loss," he mirrored back to her, and then moved away for others to take their turn.

After several others paid their respect, a woman appearing to be about the same age as the girl's mother stepped up. She took both of the mother's hands in her own, looked directly into her eyes and quietly said, "I'm so deeply sorry for your loss, Sue. Remember, I lost my Emily at about the same age. I know how you feel. I'm here for you and I promise that eventually you'll be okay. You'll never get over the loss, but you will have peace again."

The grieving mother threw her arms around the other mother's neck. They held a tight embrace for a long time and wept together. When they finally pulled apart, the girl's mother could hardly speak.

"Thank you, Beverly," was all she could muster.

"Call me when you need me. Any time, day or night, and I'll stay in touch."

"Thank you, again. I don't know what to say."

"You don't need to say anything. That's part of understanding each other. We'll talk soon," Beverly assured her again and moved over to comfort the father.

"Let's go back and talk about this," said Jeffrey's mother. A portal opened and they stepped back into her living room. Before he left, Jeffrey looked over at the little girl sitting on the coffin. She smiled and waved at him. Jeffrey smiled and waved back, then turned and disappeared in a flash of light.

∞∞∞

"What did you notice, Jeffrey?" his mother asked, once they were again seated.

"Well, people were certainly well-intentioned, each trying in his or her own way to comfort the parents; but it was the mother who had also lost a child who really made a connection," Jeffrey observed.

"Exactly. There was the power of authenticity in her words. People could say, 'I know how you feel' and as you said, were well-meaning, but it was the mother who had experienced the same loss whose words of comfort went right to the grieving mother's heart. That's a strength you'll bring to the table when you whisper to a young man who has lost his mother, or who has an alcoholic or abusive father, '*I know how you feel,*' and he'll sense that he's not alone. You'll be able to touch lives that others won't. You helped Charlotte for example, because she identified with you, both having lost a close loved one. That will be one of the blessings you'll experience as you serve, ultimately made possible by the pain you endured. That's something though seemingly impossible at the time, for which we can eventually learn gratitude."

"Remember," William added, "before being nailed to the cross, Christ suffered in Gethsemane, descending below all things. We can't comprehend how, but in that moment, He experienced everything we could possibly suffer, not only to pay for our sins and transgressions, but so He could understand and nurture us perfectly. As a result, He literally bled from every pore. What He willingly undertook, because of His love for us, means that when we feel alone, judged, misunderstood, or even hated; when we are sick or suffering in any way to any degree, there's one Being in the universe who can speak to our hearts and authentically say, *'I know how you feel. I'm here to cry with you, because I've felt it. I'm here to lift, support and comfort you. I'll bring you peace and strength, and together we can triumph over everything you'll face.'* Now *that's* something for which we can all be grateful."

They were all quiet and let the significance of that sink in.

Eventually it was William who broke the silence. "Thus, endeth the lesson on gratitude," he said. "Thank you," he nodded to Jeffrey's mother, "for adding so much to the lesson. Before we jump into the next trait, who's up for something to eat?"

"Wait a minute. Eat? You eat here?! Eat, as in food?" Jeff couldn't believe what he was hearing. "Why wasn't I told this sooner?"

"One of my favorite portals," Will responded. "And I can't wait a minute. Minutes don't exist here," he smiled. "Follow me."

Chapter Eleven

Will, Jeffrey and their parents stepped from a portal into what appeared to be a massive dining room. It reminded Jeff of a large medieval castle, with a vaulted ceiling and a huge wooden table running the length of a spacious chamber. The table was beautiful and clean, its wood lit from within. Other spirits were enjoying meals in small groups at other tables around the room.

"I can't believe you didn't tell me about eating," exclaimed Jeff. "That's practically my favorite thing to do. But it would never have occurred to me that anyone would or could eat something after dying."

"This seemed like a good moment to surprise you. And I missed the clues as well. Christ ate fish and honeycomb after his resurrection and mentioned on another occasion that he would later drink of the fruit of the vine in his Father's kingdom. In the spirit world, we don't *have* to eat. We don't get hungry, and we don't suffer negative effects when we don't eat. No one here can starve to death," Will chuckled, stating the obvious. "Eating is more of a social event, including the most delicious food you've ever had. It provides wonderful tastes and satisfaction, as though it were a real meal, but then dissipates, so there are no calories or waste. Now let's get started. Describe to me in detail your all-time favorite meal."

Jeff thought for a moment, then with his mouth practically watering as he imagined it, said, "Alaskan king crab with melted butter, a New York strip steak, corn on the cob – buttered, salted and peppered, with chocolate ice cream for dessert."

He'd never had those things in the same meal, and had only tasted king crab once, but he'd loved it and it seemed like a good choice for his first meal in the world of spirits.

But then he caught himself. "Wait! There's nothing dead here. I can't have king crab or steak. Do I have to order all vegetables?" Jeff asked in dismay.

"Come sit down," Will laughed, beckoning to a seat at the table. "How do you like your steak cooked?"

"Medium," answered Jeff cautiously, not wanting to get his hopes up.

The five sat, Jeffrey next to his mother, Will and his parents across the table. A bright silver platter appeared in front of him. On it were what seemed to be four large pods, each with a short stem at the top, as though they'd just been freshly cut from a tree or vine, each a different color. The only one Jeffrey recognized was the green husk of an ear of corn. The others: red, light brown and darker brown, weren't familiar. All were lit from within.

"Why don't you start with the light brown one," Will encouraged.

Jeff slowly picked up the knife and fork on either side of the platter and placed them on the brown pod, ready to cut into the top. He didn't have to exert any pressure. Like the rose that responded to him when he first arrived, the plant opened the moment he touched it. Steam came out, along with the smell of a perfectly cooked steak.

"You've got to be kidding me," Jeffrey exclaimed. "A vegetable steak?!"

"Try it," his mother urged.

Jeffrey took a bite of the most delicious steak he'd ever eaten – tender, juicy and hot.

"Well, what do you think?" Will asked, knowing the answer.

What came out wasn't a word, but a long, joyful moan.

"MMMMmmmmm…."

Everyone laughed and started their meals. Jeffrey almost finished the entire steak at once, then decided to try the king crab. As it was revealed in the red pod, Jeff noticed it wasn't shaped like a crab leg – more like a large lump of meat. It was sweet, already buttered and delicious. A glass of crystal, cold water refreshed him while his mother and mentor each enjoyed their salmon and swordfish. Jeff wondered what Will might say if he never wanted to leave this place.

"You'll have a hard time believing me right now," Will said, almost reading his thoughts, "because I know this is the best meal you've ever had, but there are even better things to come. Call these your transition meals. We're usually drawn at first to those foods we liked on earth, again bringing our personalities with us, but most spirits eventually wind up trying the best of all foods and cultures from around the world. It's a fascinating experience with what seems like countless possibilities. But then, just when you think you've tried it all, there are foods here that aren't even on earth. Some of the most delicious are yet to come."

"*He's right,*" Jeff thought as he nodded and bit into some crispy hot corn. "*That is hard to believe. How could anything taste better than this?*" He knew Will well enough by now however, to get a little excited about the possibilities.

Before Jeff could respond out loud, William rose to his feet and announced loudly, "While everyone continues enjoying their meal, we're going to start our discussion."

Jeffrey looked up and saw that a group of people he didn't know had joined them at the table, each with his or her own food. He had been so focused on his perfect meal that he hadn't noticed their arrival. They nodded in his direction and smiled. He was curious to know what this was about.

"One of the great blessings in the world of spirits is that we get to learn from and inspire each other. People from all walks of life, as well as all eras and generations are here." William was directly addressing Jeffrey, as the others listened in. "As I mentioned, meals here are more of a social event and often a learning one. We have different themed meals. Recently, I sat in on a discussion with some of the world's great philosophers. Together, they spanned many centuries. It was fascinating to hear what they believed on Earth, how it had evolved, and how their thinking had changed since their arrival here.

"On another occasion, I listened in on a discussion with founders of some of the world's great religions. It was riveting to hear their histories first-hand. We've enjoyed talented musicians as they played for us, and famous artists as they displayed their handiwork and shared the inspiration of each. I recently attended a lecture by Michelangelo, one of my favorites. We watched a scene of him carving the Pietà out of a single block of marble while he told his story. It was remarkable.

William continued, "Some presenters will be well-known, like Nelson Mandela, Helen Keller, Edmund Hillary, Albert Einstein, Abraham Lincoln, Harriett Tubman and others. But I think you'll find some of the most fascinating are ordinary folks who led extraordinary lives, like those you'll hear in this meeting. Typically, the ones in whom you'll be most interested at first will be those from your own culture and background, but eventually most branch out into all cultures and ages.

"To introduce the third angel trait, Jeffrey, the individuals gathered here share something in common. Keep enjoying your meal, listen and soak it all in," William smiled. "Just *be present.*"

Jeff nodded, still enjoying his meal and curious to see how this would all unfold.

A man positioned near the center of the table stood first. "You might have actually heard of me, Jeffrey, though I don't consider myself famous. I composed a hymn I believe you sang in church."

Jeffrey was trying hard to figure out who it was.

"My name is Horatio G. Spafford. This is my wife, Anna." The woman at his side smiled and nodded.

"Our events occurred mostly in the 1870's, in the United States. Our son, also here with us," he pointed to a man sitting by his wife, "died from pneumonia when he was just a little boy. The sadness of losing a child is beyond description," father and son nodded to each other, "but that wasn't the only challenge we faced. That same year, most of my business was destroyed in the great Chicago fire. I worked hard to recover, but it was difficult. I was bankrupt.

"In 1873, Anna and our four daughters were crossing the Atlantic on a large ship. I was supposed to be with them but had business in Chicago. I was to take a later ship to Europe and meet them there. We'd planned a wonderful family holiday and I was excited to see them."

As Spafford shared his story, a large three-dimensional image appeared over the center of the table, displaying what he now was describing. Jeffrey could see through the suspended vision, so he was still connected with everyone around the table and at the same time, could see the story come to life as it unfolded. He loved these spirit world surprises as they popped up.

Horatio continued. "Anna's ship hit another ship and sank. She was barely able to cling to a piece of the wreckage…" An image appeared of Horatio's wife, desperately hanging onto a piece of floating wood, screaming and sobbing for her children. Jeffrey noticed Anna, across from him, wiping away tears. The story went on. "She was rescued by someone in a small boat, but our girls died – all four of them together. They too, are here with us now."

Four young women sitting by the son raised their hands. One did a little wave.

"I said that the pain of losing my son was terrible. Now, losing all of our daughters, and at the same time was so overwhelming, so unfathomable." He paused and a glow filled his countenance. "Thank God we've been reunited." His family smiled and lit up, as well.

He continued his story. "I caught the next available ship, anxious to be with my wife. A few days into the journey, the captain tenderly let me know we were in the same spot where the ship had gone down, where the bodies of my beautiful girls were. It was at that moment I was inspired to write a hymn – one you've sung in church, *'It is Well with My Soul,'* that, as I understand, has inspired others on Earth in times of need. Through tragedy, I'm grateful to say, I was able to keep moving forward and create something that could help others, and I thank God for that revelation." He paused a moment and sat down.

William waited for the words to sink in, then thanked Horatio for his story and acknowledged that it was wonderful to have his entire family there. "I asked Brother

Spafford to start us out because, as most of you know, we usually begin these meetings with a hymn. With his experience fresh in mind, let us sing, '*It is Well with My Soul.*'"

Lovely piano and string accompaniment started from somewhere. The lyrics appeared on the screen over the table. But this wasn't simply a rendition of a hymn that Jeffrey was used to in church. Because of the richness of music in the spirit world, and because everyone knew the background and felt the emotions of Spafford's first-hand experience, this truly came from the heart. It was a touching and unifying moment for all who were there.

> *When peace like a river attendeth my way,*
>
> *When sorrows like sea billows roll*
>
> *Whatever my lot, Thou hast taught me to say,*
>
> *It is well, it is well with my soul.*[1]

A prayer was offered by another guest, thanking God for the food they had enjoyed and inviting His Spirit to preside over the meeting. Then one by one, other participants stood and shared their stories.

---

[1] TEXT BY HORATIO G. SPAFFORD

One spirit's wife on Earth had abandoned him, causing him to raise their toddler on his own. He'd later remarried, then lost that wife and newborn baby in an accident. He'd still prevailed, married once again and raised a beautiful family. All were at the table and introduced themselves to the group, acknowledging their loving father and his significant role and influence in their lives.

Another had been rushing to an appointment and had accidentally backed over her youngest son with her car. The tragedy of losing the boy was magnified by her sorrow of having caused his death. She exercised faith and perseverance, recovered as best she could and raised her family, most of whom were still on Earth. Here she was with the son who had died, holding hands and smiling while telling their story.

Not all stories involved death. One young woman was a strong hopeful for the Winter Olympics. She had gone off the road in a car accident and was paralyzed from the waist-down. Working hard to overcome this challenge, she became a world-class wheelchair marathon racer. The scenes of her on the screen not only showed some of her racing victories but showed her in various aspects of her life. Her exuberant smile and energetic spirit made everyone around her happy. Her joy was infectious.

"Jeffrey, the next angel trait, in addition to *Be Present* and *Be Grateful,* is to **Move Forward**. You've heard some great examples of those that did and the impact it had on their lives and others. We'll soon see examples in other's lives as well as your own, when people didn't move forward - what held them back and the impact it had on their lives, their self-esteem and ultimately their light and happiness. I'd remind you; this is not to judge anyone but to learn from their examples and then lovingly nudge and inspire them to keep moving forward.

"First, there's a critical thing you haven't done." William's demeanor changed. He said sternly, "Frankly, I'm a bit disappointed."

Jeffrey was startled by the shift and saw that everyone around the table was looking at him. What had he missed?

"My friend, you didn't eat your ice cream!"

Everyone laughed together. Jeffrey sighed with relief, then used his spoon to touch the top of the remaining pod. The dark brown pod opened, and Jeff tasted the best chocolate ice cream he'd ever had, still frozen and perfect in every way.

As the conversation around the table died down and the last bit of ice cream was scraped from its container, Jeff and Will caught each other's attention, stood and thanked everyone, and the two were off to Earth.

Chapter Twelve

As Jeff and Will returned from their mission, they were in a location of William's choosing – a tropical paradise in Paradise. Crystal blue waters shimmered with light, pristine white sand beaches seemed to stretch on forever, small islands covered with various deep green plants dotted the ocean, palm trees towering above.

They stood for a while without speaking and took it all in. Jeff finally broke the silence and asked something that had been confusing him as they'd jumped from location to location for his customized classrooms.

"Billions have lived and died on Earth and I now understand, on other earths. To see a beach of this beauty completely empty doesn't make sense, not only as a desirable destination for others, but from sheer numbers. Where is everyone?"

"Good question. There's literally limitless space here in the world of spirits. In that regard, the term 'world' is a misnomer, implying a round sphere like Earth. This world extends throughout the universe. Spirits enter it from Earth and from the numerous other planets Father has created, so there are many more individuals here than billions, trillions or more. If we'd wanted, we could have gone to a beach where many are gathered enjoying each other. The portals we use make an infinite area rather small, if you will, or at least, all-accessible. We can go anywhere we need to in just moments and either be with a lot of spirits or just the two of us. Because this is your classroom right now, I chose the latter, thinking it would be easier to be fully present."

As mind-boggling as that was, because Jeffrey had used the various portals, it made complete sense. He simply nodded. *I had such a limited perspective on Earth*, he thought to himself. *I never dreamed…*

"For my thoughts are not your thoughts; neither are your ways my ways,"[2] William quoted, guessing accurately what Jeffrey was thinking. He too, had been humbled by it all as he'd adjusted to this spiritual paradise.

They sat down in the sand to continue their discussion, the foam of the breaking waves dissipating just a couple yards from their feet.

"Tell me what you observed about moving forward, as we watched different people on Earth."

The two had just finished what they had done before to share *'be present'* and *'be grateful'* – examining some mortals moving forward and others not, as well as seeing the impact

---

[2] ISAIAH 55:8

and degrees of light involved in each situation. Unlike the more dramatic stories they'd heard at what Jeffrey dubbed "the feast," most of these were simple day-to-day examples.

They'd observed two parents with a young family who'd recently added twins. Though it would never make it in a history book or even be known outside that community, the day-to-day caring for four young children, which seemed overwhelming at times, was a sublime example of these parents moving forward together. Friends and loved ones who were sensitive enough to help were also blessed through their service. Sometimes moving forward was to help others move forward as well.

For another set of parents, an autistic child commanded their attention. Their efforts, though difficult, yet consistent day-to-day, were blessed as they each strengthened their spiritual core and helped their struggling son slowly progress.

In some instances, suggesting to someone to step back and let someone else solve their own challenge by him or herself ultimately helped both move forward most effectively. Jeffrey learned he had to really pay attention to know what the situation warranted as to how and when he would nudge someone through a loving whisper.

Will arranged for them to observe people facing basically the same challenge, but with different responses. Some, in the face of adversity complained, blamed others, made excuses, or simply hoped that things would somehow magically change. But they stayed stuck and even appeared to regress in their growth and light.

Others facing similar circumstances were also frustrated and sometimes angered by the situation. But at some point, they dug deep, confronted the challenge, got creative and energized, and overcame or at least minimized the problem. These folks seemed to develop a resilience that would help them get stronger, face even greater challenges and ultimately live happier more fulfilled lives.

Jeffrey had been shown two young men about the same age in very different circumstances. One, though physically able to work, had become dependent on others taking care of him. Though he'd expressed to friends that he loved being able to hang out and avoid work, he and his inner light seemed to be languishing. It was having a detrimental impact on the core of who he was as a son of God. The other had so many physical disabilities that he was only able to pull a handle on a machine in an assembly line, but he showed up every day with pride and a sense of contribution. As a result, he was glowing with self-esteem and was clearly in his own humble way, moving forward.

In each instance and in other examples when they saw someone who looked discouraged or down, they had encouragingly said, *"Move forward,"* or in some instances simply, *"Keep moving."* Those that listened literally lifted their heads and appeared to get a boost of energy. Others, for whatever reason, weren't yet ready to take that step. As before, there was no judgment on the part of the heavenly messengers – just patience and understanding as they knew they would visit them again when they might be ready to hear their support.

William used one example to show multiple angel traits at work. They observed a husband and wife at the dinner table eating while watching the news. The lead story showed some islands that had been devastated by a hurricane. People were having a difficult time getting water, food and other necessary supplies to survive. Will watched the situation for a couple of minutes, then gently said, *"be grateful"* to the two. In just seconds, the man muted the television and said to his spouse, "You know, watching this, it's not lost on me that I just poured a glass of cold water without thinking about it. We're having a nice dinner and we have a refrigerator and cupboards full of just about everything we need."

"I was thinking the same thing. I feel so bad for all those people," said the wife sympathetically.

Sensing they were in a good state of mind to hear it, Will followed with, *"move forward."*

The wife continued, "But what can we do? I feel so helpless when I see them suffer."

The husband got up and brought his laptop to the table. "What do you say we make a contribution to a relief agency, to someone we know will help?"

Jeffrey and Will watched as the couple made a contribution to a disaster relief fund. Taking action moved their souls forward and would help those in need move forward, as well.

After seeing other examples, it was time to return. Jeffrey began to summarize his experiences as they sat in this strikingly beautiful classroom.

"I remember when I first heard *'be present',* I thought it was about listening to others. I've since realized that being present is multi-faceted. Yes, it can involve listening, but it can also involve judgment and expectations; being present with a person or with a task, alone with our own thinking or even with Father in prayer. It seems there are many ways to experience being or not being present.

"I see 'move forward' just as multi-faceted," he continued. "People move forward in their own way, at their own pace, with their own unique challenges. And it's not a competition. It's very personalized. Think of that one rich guy we observed who was headed down such an ugly path. By the world's standards he moved backward by risking his fame and reputation when he entered rehab to get his life back on track. Yet, by seemingly moving backward, he moved forward, was filled with light and became an example to others who were struggling. I can tell he'll have to stay humble and not get caught up in the fame of his recovery, but even that will be moving forward in his own way."

William smiled at the depth of his student's observations. Jeffrey had grown a great deal since he'd entered this spiritual domain.

"In contrast to that guy's wealth," Jeff continued, "we observed that one woman living alone in a hut. She had nothing but a mat on the floor and yet exuded more light than just about anyone I've seen. I saw joy and contentment in her life. She seemed to be moving forward with each simple act of kindness and love for those around her. What a remarkable woman! I don't see anything inherently wrong with money. The key seems to be whether you bless those around you with whatever you have.

"One situation I hadn't considered were those who struggled with mental health. For them, there was still a path to move forward, but part of it was in seeking assistance from others including medical help and counseling to better move forward in the most productive way."

"You're spot on," responded Will. "Pulling it all together, I've found that *'be present'* and *'move forward'* tie into each other in a critical way. As we quiet our minds and are fully present, all of us as God's children receive promptings as to our own next best step forward. It's remarkable and humbling that there are about eight billion different next steps. There is one for each person on Earth, as well as countless promptings here in the spirit world...a personalized, loving formula from a perfect Father. When we heed those promptings and follow through, there's a feeling of accomplishment, of inner strength and light, as well as happiness and fulfillment. Then we can each *express gratitude,* our other angel trait, to Father for those promptings and for the strength to follow through and prevail. You know by now that it often isn't easy, and is sometimes even extremely difficult, but that's how we grow and ultimately become more Christ-like.

"Building on that thought," Will continued, "I'd like you to see something in your life portal. We're going to review a series of accomplishments, all of them small steps in your progression. I want you to focus on your mother's reaction as you achieved each one, sometimes even falteringly."

The two moved into Jeffrey's portal and watched brief moments that added to who he was. They started with him learning how to walk and talk, being taught how to read and acquiring new skill sets. They saw activities like sports, learning to play the piano, helping with chores, completing school assignments and doing something nice for someone. They even watched moments of accomplishment after Jeffrey's mom had died and was supporting him from her vantage point in the spirit world. They then returned and sat on the beach.

"What did you notice about your mom's reactions? Even in simple moments, like you taking your first steps?"

"She was overjoyed. She would clap, cheer and help or encourage me to try it again. You could see the delight in her face. Even when I stumbled, she was nudging me along, confident that I could do it."

"Your mother really loves you and delights in anything you do to move forward. The same is true for Father, though infinitely more so. Everything He does and asks of us is pointed toward our eternal joy and growth. Even His commandments, which some view as limiting or a burden, are exactly the opposite of that. They're meant for our development, self-discipline and progress – for *moving forward*. And all because of His perfect love for each and every one of us."

The two sat reflecting on the beach for a while, the only sound the lapping of waves on the shore and the occasional seagull squawking greetings overhead.

William finally looked over and asked, "Ready for your next topic?"

"Would we have to leave this?" Jeffrey asked, a bit dismayed.

"You can always come back. What would you consider to be one of the most interesting moments in history?" Will inquired.

"History as in U.S. history, world history, my life's history?"

"Whatever comes to mind when you think of fascinating moments," he answered. He seemed deliberately vague, so Jeffrey ventured a guess.

"Well…I'm not much of a history buff, but I guess I'd have to say the U.S. Civil War has always been intriguing to me. I watched a mini-series on it once and it was fascinating." Jeffrey paused. "Is it a problem that I'm picking a war when we're here in this peaceful environment?"

"Not at all," said Will. "I appreciate your sensitivity to that. Wars are rich with examples of studying the human condition. You'll see hatred, fear, anger, ugliness, depression and of course, extreme pain and death. On the other hand, you'll see examples of courage and bravery, compassion, sacrifice, perseverance, and even love.

"To introduce the next angel trait, let's go back to one of the pivotal moments of the U.S. Civil War, the battle at Gettysburg."

Chapter Thirteen

Jeffrey and Will landed in the middle of a raging battle, chaos all around. There were men yelling and guns being fired. Thick smoke filled the air, and the sounds of injured soldiers screaming and cannons booming in the distance could be heard. The two were standing on top of the hill known as Little Round Top near Gettysburg, Pennsylvania. One solder yelled and pointed his gun directly at Jeff, making him duck. The man fired and the lead ball hit someone directly behind him. *This was terrifying!* Jeff wasn't sure where to stand or what to do.

"Pause!" said Will. The entire scene around them stopped, everything holding exactly as it was, a profound silence now filling the air. Jeffrey noticed that one soldier who had just jumped over a log was suspended in mid-air.

"This isn't a movie or a reenactment. It's the real thing. You're seeing a 3-dimensional recording of the actual battle of Gettysburg."

"This is really incredible!" Jeffrey exclaimed, pulling himself together.

"It takes getting used to in extreme circumstances like war. I saw you duck," Will noted. "But you can freeze motion and walk around, slow everything down, even back it up. This and scenes like these from throughout history can be some of the greatest learning environments you'll ever experience. We can go as far back in Earth's history as you'd like, up to the point where things are now and everything in between. We can go to the depths of the ocean, the tops of mountains, or even walk with Armstrong on the moon. Now watch this.

"Commentary," said Will.

"At this point in the battle," explained a narrator, the voice seemingly coming from nowhere and everywhere, *"the Southern forces were charging the hill. Colonel Chamberlain and his men were running out of ammunition. If the rebels captured Little Round Top, they would be able to flank the Northern soldiers and cause a crushing defeat, perhaps even ending the war with a rebel victory."*

"Continue," ordered Will. The scene came back to life. The soldier suspended in front of them fell to the ground, then scrambled to take cover.

"Bayonet!" yelled someone loudly behind them.

The narrator continued over the din, *"Yelling an order that no one expected, Chamberlain commanded his weak forces to do the unthinkable – to charge."*

The 20th Maine Infantry quickly grabbed their bayonets, sliding the rings over each rifle barrel and locked them into place. Then, screaming at the top of their lungs, charged down the hill. The opposing forces, though they had strength in numbers, were so surprised they dropped their guns and threw up their arms in surrender.

"Reverse to moment of charge," Will said.

Everything around them went in reverse. One man that Jeff had stepped behind as he'd charged by going down the hill went right through him in reverse.

"Watch that soldier after they fix bayonets," William said, pointing. "Play."

The man they were looking at drew his sword, yelled, "Charge!" and rushed forward.

"Pause," stated Will again and everything stopped. "Notice that everyone around him is frozen in fear. Chamberlain yelled the order, but if this one soldier hadn't bravely taken the lead, the other soldiers might not have charged. The Confederate forces were only about thirty yards away. This one man played a key role in the Union's success and possibly changed history."

"Insight," said Will loudly.

A voice came from within the frozen soldier. *"I was simply acting on my orders. I'd heard the Colonel yell for us to charge and was trained to do what I was told, however frightening it was. It turned out to be a decisive moment for the entire war, but I had no way of knowing that at the time. My adrenalin was pumping, and I instinctively did what I was told. I'm grateful it turned out the way it did."*

"Those thoughts were recorded when this soldier entered the spirit world years later," Will clarified. "We could even ask him, Chamberlain or any of the others here to interview them – to walk through the battle step by step. Each has a story to tell. This is *the* comprehensive classroom Jeffrey, with our Earth's complete history available for our understanding. Do you get a sense of the possibilities?"

"Truly amazing, and very cool," responded Jeffrey.

"Hold that thought and come with me. We're jumping ahead several weeks."

The two found themselves in a hallway in a home in what Will clarified was South Carolina. They were standing at the bottom of some stairs near the front entrance. Two messengers in military uniform walked up the path, came to the door and knocked. A woman in a long, full dress wiping her hands on a dish towel came down the hall. She opened the door and seeing the grim looks of the two men, realized what they were about to say. She cried out and fell to the floor sobbing. Three young children ran excitedly down the stairs. When they saw their mommy crying, they ran to her and also started crying, not even sure why. Jeffrey and Will, realizing what they were seeing, were touched.

"This is the family of just one of tens-of-thousands of soldiers killed at Gettysburg. They're receiving news of their beloved's death. These children will grow up without a father and will struggle tremendously. Their mother will have a very hard life." He paused. "To be specific, fifty thousand, four hundred and seventy-two soldiers were killed over those three days and another thirty-three thousand, six hundred and sixteen were wounded. Many of them were hurt very seriously, including loss of limbs, to say nothing of the emotional damage for them and their loved ones. Project the mourning and suffering you're seeing here across the country, to all those families and loved ones over many years."

Will paused for effect, then continued, "You described the battle as *'amazing and cool.'* I understand why you said that. Would this change how you would describe what you saw?"

William didn't ask this in a condemning or judgmental way. In fact, it was with love and understanding. Still, Jeffrey felt like a knife pierced his heart.

"I didn't mean anything offensive by it," Jeff said quietly. "I hope you know that."

"I do know that Jeffrey. You've got a great heart. One of the challenges of this generation is that we've become desensitized to violence. There's nothing wrong with being excited, even intrigued to learn this way, and of course not all of history is about war and suffering. I just want to make sure you are always looking through the lens of impact and compassion as you review these events. It's helpful to know that this family has long since been reunited and the war and its aftermath are but a distant memory. But, for you to really 'get' the people you're serving, you've got to remember each challenge they face is very real for them. These aren't special effects in a movie."

Jeff was thinking hard. "I feel like I'm stating the obvious, but there's clearly a difference between how death is viewed on Earth and how it's viewed here in the spirit world. In mortality, death is most often viewed with fear and tremendous sadness. Here, because everyone has already experienced it, it's just a moment we passed over – one of relief, peace and joy.

"You're right. Because all here have experienced death, we see it completely different than those on Earth. We can talk about it easily, learn from it and be fascinated by it. We may even laugh at it at times, because of that perspective. What we can't do, if we're going to serve those on Earth most effectively, is to just be on autopilot. We need to be very thoughtful to everyone who is involved and impacted, especially since it's not as scary for us now as it still is for them. Make sense?"

Jeffrey nodded, still reflecting on the implications.

"Let's go a step further with your question. I have something very important to show you. We're going back to the battlefield. You're about to see what I think is one of the most remarkable aspects of the spirit world."

They landed in the same location in Gettysburg, but this time positioned above the scene. From this viewpoint, they could see hundreds, even thousands of soldiers beneath them on all sides, frozen in the midst of battle. Jeffrey was so intrigued with this view that he wasn't even bothered by the height at which they were hovering.

"View angels," directed Will. Suddenly, what seemed to be thousands of heavenly beings appeared, interspersed amongst the fighters. The contrast of the grittiness and darkness, with bright personages mixed throughout was stark.

"Am I seeing what I think I'm seeing? Those are all angels, right?" Jeffrey asked.

"This is what Gettysburg actually looked like for those who are able to see both the mortals involved and the attending spirits. You are seeing three of the four basic kinds of angels. The first, Guardian Angels, are assigned to do just that – guard an individual if his or her life is to be protected, or to usher them to the other side if it's their time to pass. Guardians are very much in tune with the Spirit, to know when to spare lives or bring them to the spirit world. Interestingly, they almost never understand the 'why' someone is left here or taken – that's God's ultimate plan for each of us. Their task is to protect when called on, or to lovingly bring that spirit home.

"The second kind of angel is a Comforter. I've mentioned it to you before, but just as God is there for each of us when needed, He wants us to learn to be there for each other. See that wounded soldier there with the two angels sitting next to him?" asked William, pointing below.

"Those are Comforters?"

"Yes, one is his grandfather, who passed years earlier. The other is a volunteer comforter who suffered the same injury in an earlier war. All of our comforters are either related to the person in need, close friends or experienced the same challenge themselves."

"That makes sense," Jeff nodded.

"Yes as much as we'd like to think so, or as well-intended as we are, you and I are not capable of fully comprehending the fear, pain or intense suffering someone experiences unless we have lived it ourselves. Even with the Experience Portal at our disposal, which is very powerful as you know, we've found it is most effective to involve loved ones or those who went through that same situation themselves. There are countless mortals who receive whatever support they can on Earth and subconsciously sense our love and support on this side. Literally, no one is ever truly alone. When you had your car accident, your sweet mother never left your hospital room. She was by your side until the day you were released and stayed close to encourage you through rehab. That probably doesn't surprise you."

Jeff simply smiled and shook his head in gratitude.

"Back to the battle. When soldiers are killed, not only are we there to greet them, but comforters are also sent to their loved ones to sustain them during their time of suffering. Those Comforters might even include the one who passed on. This network of angels reaches everyone. The husband of the family we just saw stayed close to them throughout their lives. Things remained difficult, but there were critical times when they felt his influence and caring."

"It's wonderful to know that." Jeffrey paused, touched by the scope of what he was starting to understand. "You mentioned four types of angels. What are the other two? I assume you're one of the others."

"Yes, though sometimes roles overlap. We're the Volunteers who share angel traits with the world. As you know by now, sometimes we're able to influence our brothers and sisters, and sometimes not so much. These traits are a gift, but it's always up to them. In reality, we're growing as much or more than those we try to influence just by staying in service. If they do respond, all are doubly blessed.

"The fourth kind of angel is that of the highest order – the Angels of the Kingdom. They are under direct command from Father and reveal gospel truths, like revelations to prophets. Angel Gabriel and those who ushered in the birth of Christ are examples of those heavenly messengers."

"I would assume that those angels are the most important, right?"

"Absolutely, but all work together to ultimately bring us closer to Father and to live more Christ-like lives. Commandments from a perfect, all-knowing Father are designed to guide and even save us. They are paramount in doing His will. On the other hand, our angel traits act as enablers to help others live those commandments," William clarified. "I'm commanded, for example, to love my neighbor as myself. When I practice being fully present with those around me, it helps me truly listen for understanding, in order to better identify and help meet their needs. Make sense?"

"It does. I'm just blown away by the scope of activities in this phase of life. It's something I never imagined."

"I've felt that way many times," Will responded. "The scope of Father's love and His plan for us is almost incomprehensible. Coming back to our learning portals, we've been witnessing an event from the 1800's, but current events are accessible as well. As things unfold on Earth, we can see and review them here to determine what's really going on. In some cases, there are those focused on negative, sometimes evil designs and think no one knows. We're able to review their actions from different perspectives, then do our best to influence them to change the course of what they are doing. We nudge them to hopefully do the right thing and if that fails, as it often does, we inspire others to change and perhaps minimize the results. It's an interesting process, to say the least."

"It seems rather daunting," Jeff replied. "How do you know where to start?"

"We simply give it our best shot, however falteringly, just as they do on Earth," Will explained. "Though we have clear advantages over mortals, such as the portals and learning from scenes like the one before you now, we still can't do it all. Father is ultimately in charge and is aware of literally everything going on. He guides us through impressions but remember that humans have their agency and can still choose evil. Those of us assigned to Earth strive to heed His promptings. It isn't perfect, but it's the best we can do.

"As I mentioned, not all history is tragic like war. I'd like to share with you some simple 'slice of life' moments that are some of my favorites."

The two found themselves in a modern-day home where a father was singing a lullaby to three young children he'd just tucked into bed. He didn't have a great voice. It just came from his heart. Jeffrey noticed other spirits in the room enjoying this tender moment.

"I chose this scene for you because he's a direct descendent of mine. It won't make any history books," Will said quietly as the man finished singing, then kissed each child and left the room. "These moments remind me of the goodness that is out there, in contrast to other scenes you'll see. They help keep us centered. Such love."

In another scene, a worried mother wrote online that though many had been invited, only one child was coming to her autistic son's birthday party. The local high school football team heard about it and together came to the celebration.

The joy on the young boy's face as his local heroes showed up warmed the onlookers' hearts.

They observed someone reaching out to someone who was alone and depressed, a coach taking extra time after practice to help a struggling student, a couple really listening to understand each other and healing after an argument. These were the kinds of things that made their spirits beam brightly.

In addition to personal interactions, Jeffrey was shown interesting key moments of invention – the telephone, television, lightbulb, computer, and even the early development of his favorite sports. He realized there was no end to what could be observed and learned with literally every historic moment captured here.

Jeff was trying to soak it all in. "This is fascinating, humbling and inspiring all at once. How do you not just always stay here studying history when it's brought to life like this? How do you get anything else done?"

"You have to keep the key purpose in mind. You and I will use this learning portal to study human nature, so we can more effectively influence mortals on Earth," Will responded. "I want to be where I can help others move forward as much and as often as possible.

"I have one more to show you, which I've saved for last," said Will. "This was a dear friend of mine I knew on Earth. It's a popular replay for many of us. It occurred on another battlefield."

The two traveled to the 1960's and found themselves standing over two soldiers. One of them was clearly badly wounded, appearing close to death. They soon determined that the soldiers couldn't speak a word of the other's language. The dying Vietnamese soldier slowly pulled a picture of his family out of his pocket. He pointed to each image, struggling to say something about each one. The American soldier, realizing what was being communicated, listened as best he could, then pulled out a picture of his family and said a few words. He then held the picture over his heart. The enemy soldier looked up and into the eyes of the American; smiled and nodded his head, placing his hand with the picture of his family over his heart and passed away. They watched as he was lovingly ushered into the spirit world.

"They're now the dearest of friends," added Will, after a long pause. "I'd love to introduce you sometime."

"Wow," said Jeffrey. "That was unexpected." He took a deep breath to get his composure. "I'd love to meet them. I'll never forget that."

"Let's introduce angel trait number four. Remember these aren't in any specific order. Each is important to the person we're trying to inspire in that moment. *Moving forward* for one might be as important as *being present* for another or *being grateful* for a third, or even a combination of those depending on what the person is facing. I did save this one for last because of its nuances. It starts out pretty basic, then goes quite deep as you continue to explore it. In a way, all of these principles do – you can learn something new about them every time you are open to it – but this is one of my favorites."

Will continued by asking, "How have you felt while we've been watching these different events, from the Civil War down to my friends in Vietnam?"

"Fascinated, intrigued, saddened by the ugliness, and inspired by the unseen angel support. I'll never forget seeing two supposed enemies sharing family pictures with each other at such a tender moment. That was very touching."

"It's a wonderful part of who you are Jeffrey. You seem delighted and intrigued by life in general. The fourth angel trait is to **Stay Curious**. It starts with what you're exemplifying right now, and really have been since you arrived – what we call a growth mindset. It involves a willingness to learn and to keep learning throughout our lives. It's having the humility to acknowledge that we have room to improve.

"Father sent us here to grow, learn and progress, so a curious mind is a valuable, even critical trait. Some of the events we've just witnessed were chosen to lift our spirits, others to enhance learning; some to deepen our compassion; yet all are helping us to grow in different ways as long as we keep a curious mind open to the possibilities. Based on your response, I suspect I'd have a hard time keeping you out of these learning portals which is great. I don't take that for granted. There are spirits here who won't watch an historical event, because it doesn't support their point of view of what happened."

"Wait…you're telling me that there are spirits who can witness what actually happened – see the event as it really occurred and even hear that person talk about it – and they refuse because it won't justify their beliefs? How is that possible?"

"Human nature, including spirit nature, is a funny thing Jeffrey. People often believe what they want to believe, even with actual evidence to the contrary. Your open, curious mindset will help you grow in leaps and bounds, as you take advantage of the tools we have at our disposal.

"Soon we'll go deeper with this principle, but first I have something inspiring I want you to see. Not all events that lift us need to be in replay. Follow me."

Chapter Fourteen

Teacher and student moved to a hill overlooking a location familiar to Jeffrey. It was the spot where he first arrived in the spirit world after the initial reunion with his mother and extended family.

Jeffrey smiled as he thought back, "I'll never forget my first view of this amazing place. The homes, the flowers, the lake and mountains in the distance, the entire landscape took my breath away. It's still stunning."

"It was a beautiful moment," Will agreed. "I'm still struck by it, as well. We're here because of a special arrival. Even with all the glories surrounding us, what you are about to witness is one of the most joyful experiences for everyone here. Many will observe this moment through portals, but I wanted you here in person. Watch that space right by the garden where that crowd is gathering." He pointed to a spot below. "The woman arriving just died on Earth. She is finishing her family reunion and will be here momentarily. Here's the best part. This woman has been blind her entire life. She lived almost ninety-four years without seeing a thing. Watch her reaction when she sees this setting."

Just then a portal opened, and a group of spirits stepped out together. Three in front included the new arrival, a man holding her hand who Will identified as her husband, and the other woman, her welcoming angel. They were followed closely by a couple who Jeffrey learned, were the woman's parents. She had just seen them all moments before for the first time. As she did, Will reported, she instinctively reached out and held each loved one's face with both hands, lightly touching their cheeks, nose and forehead, as though she couldn't quite trust what her restored eyes were seeing. She cried out with recognition, then held each in a tight embrace.

Stepping into the garden, the woman saw the town and splendor of nature surrounding it. She stood there frozen in amazement, her mouth literally gaping open, her eyes looking all around trying to soak it in, trying to comprehend what her newfound sense was revealing. Tears were streaming down her face. She turned and threw her arms around her husband, who was also weeping, hugging him for a long time.

They then watched as the new arrival started taking in this beautiful world, touching everything as she connected the feeling with what she was now seeing for the first time. Jeff and Will sat there soaking in this sacred event. The accompanying glow was one of the brightest moments Jeff had seen since his arrival.

"You can see why these will be some of your favorite moments," Will finally said. "All arrivals are fun to watch; but those who were blind who now see, deaf who now hear, crippled who now walk, those who lost limbs now restored are some of the most touching. One woman passed over recently who'd had Parkinson's disease. She had a remarkable singing voice that she lost when she became ill. Once she realized her voice had been healed on arrival, she didn't hold back. She sang a song on the spot that was one of the most beautiful things I've ever heard."

"Sounds remarkable," said Jeffrey.

Will beckoned to Jeff to sit on the lawn.

"While we're here, let's relax and explore the trait of *staying curious* at a deeper level. Genuine curiosity is about much more than learning. Remember how you felt when you were watching the dad who was ignoring his daughter while watching the football game. I recall you labeled him a 'jerk.' Tell me more about how you felt watching him."

"The dad was being rude to his little girl, plain and simple. I don't do well with that."

"I get it. Hold that thought. I want you to watch a scene from about thirty years before 'TV-dad' and tell me what you notice."

The scenery shifted around them. The town disappeared and they found themselves watching a young boy in his bedroom playing with his toys. Suddenly, his head popped up. He heard his dad coming down the hall. He looked scared and ran into his closet.

"Jeremy!" yelled the dad. "Jeremy!" he yelled louder coming into the room. He heard a sound from the closet. "If you don't get your butt out here right now, I'll beat it until you don't have one to sit on!"

The little boy slowly came out of the closet, but too slow for the dad. He grabbed the child's arm and threw him to the floor. Jeffrey almost lunged at the man to stop him.

"This happened a long time ago," assured Will. "It's ugly, but keep in mind you're watching a replay."

"Why were you in the closet?" the dad bellowed. "And don't lie to me, boy."

"I was scared," the child answered timidly.

"Scared of what?" The little boy struggled to find an answer. It was clear he didn't dare identify the real source of his fear.

The father didn't wait for an answer. "I'll give you something to be scared about!" He proceeded to grab the child, put him over his knees with one arm, then reached with his other arm and took off his belt. The little boy was screaming as the father raised the belt.

"That's enough!" Jeffrey yelled. "I get it. Why are we watching this?"

Just before the dad's arm came down, Will directed the scene to "Freeze!" The father was motionless with his belt mid-air, the little boy mid-squirm, mid-scream, trying to get away. "The boy you're looking at is the little girl's father who was watching the football game."

It took a moment for Jeffrey to absorb what Will had just said. "You mean that Jeremy grows up to be the little girl's father?"

"That's right," said Will. "Jeremy was raised by a single dad who was abusive, who sadly, was also beaten by his father. To his credit, Jeremy, though he's gruff and distant, has never struck his daughter. He has at least been able to stop the physical cycle of abuse. We're still working with him on being a better dad and demonstrating more love. How does that make you feel toward Jeremy now?"

Jeff was silent.

"To be clear," Will declared, "we do *not* condone any form of abuse, physical or mental – period. These are amongst our most difficult situations. First, because of the pain and suffering of the victim, but also because the abuser will pay a terrible price at judgment day if he or she doesn't change and repent. The immediate priority is the safety of the child through whatever means we can influence, but it's hard to get through. We often don't succeed, but we don't give up. When we do reach someone like we did Jeremy, who's still making progress, it's critically important both for the victim and the abuser. Both are children of God.

"Jeremy has a long way to go in becoming a better father, but we'll continue to encourage him in every way we can to change his thinking and behavior. It will be hard for him to hear what we're saying, but if what he senses is negative – that we hate him – he has less a chance of hearing our promptings. The more loving we are while still being very direct, the better chance he has of listening and that includes being more receptive to Father's promptings. Remember we're not alone in this effort. God is still the primary Source of inspiration and the ultimate Judge of all.

"There's an important underlying principle here that ties to *staying curious* that I want you to remember. Right or wrong, people do what makes sense to them, given their current thinking and beliefs."

"Right or wrong, people do what makes sense to them, given their thinking and beliefs," repeated Jeffrey.

Will nodded. "If someone does something that leaves me baffled or upset, if I *stay curious* and try to see why it made sense to them, it helps me keep perspective and see more options than just getting angry or lashing out. I'm in a better state of mind to deal with it more effectively. Again, we don't condone bad behavior. Justice needs to be served and people need to be protected. *Staying curious* to really understand helps us be at our best – a healthier helper, if you will – so we know how to deal with the situation most effectively.

"Here's an interesting example of this," Will continued. "Let me know what you think. The manager is someone I know personally."

They watched the scene change and witnessed a young man, about 18-years-old, getting caught stealing money from a register in the department store where he was working. The manager, wanting to make an example of the rogue employee, not only fired him on the spot, but screamed at and berated him in front of the other employees. He then called the police and after filing a report with the officers, had the now ex-employee escorted from the store.

Just as the young man was being taken off in a police car, the manager looking on, Will froze the scene and asked Jeff his opinion.

"I'm not sure about this one," responded Jeffrey. "On one hand, the boss had every right to fire the young man. If he overlooked it, others might be encouraged to steal from him. I've worked retail as you know and suspect that the young man would have been warned the day he was hired about some sort of zero-tolerance policy most stores have against theft."

"Everything you've said is accurate," said Will. "Go on," he encouraged.

"Well, in this case I think he should have been fired but screaming at him and bringing the police in seemed excessive. Again, on the other hand, you can't overlook the fact that he stole the money. I'm torn. What am I missing?"

"Let's let the boss tell us. He's since passed over and has recorded his thoughts for us. Insight," Will commanded.

"I wish I'd known about the power of staying curious when I fired this young man," Jeff heard the manager say as he looked at him frozen, his face in an angry scowl. *"One of the unintended consequences of me yelling at him was that my remaining employees lived in fear of me from that time forward. They'd never seen that side of me. If I had it to do over, I would have still fired him, but this was a young man just starting his career. I'd want to know why it made sense to steal from me when I helped him out as I had. I would*

have sought out his parents and helped him get counseling, instead of giving him a police record, which made it difficult for him to turn things around."

Will jumped in. "Pause. It's significant that he said he still would have fired the young man. *Staying curious* doesn't mean we simply shrug off bad behavior and ignore it. In fact, it actually doesn't have anything to do with the other person. It's all about us and our thinking. This angel trait keeps us in a healthy, genuinely curious state of mind so we're at our best to deal with the situation. In this case, the man would have kept to his store policy and fired him, which he needed to do, but the compassion that came later, as he reflected on how he handled it might have led to a better outcome for the young man, the other employees and ultimately for the manager himself. Make sense?"

"I think so," Jeffrey responded slowly, feeling as though he might just be scratching the surface with this particular trait.

"We can go even deeper. I've seen this play out in much more difficult situations. In one case, a father's only child was murdered by a young gang member. It literally took years, but after intense mourning and mental anguish, he started to get curious as to why a young boy would commit murder. He looked into it and found that the boy had a traumatic childhood, including being orphaned at a young age. His grandfather raised him as best he could, but it had been a struggle."

Will continued, "The father met with the grandfather and found he was grieving deeply. He'd tried to raise the boy with good morals, but the boy had succumbed to peer pressure. That's why he'd killed someone as initiation to a gang. It was his need to feel accepted. As he learned more, curiosity led to compassion, which led to forgiveness. The father and grandfather together have influenced countless others to avoid gangs and have hope for a better future. The boy still served a prison sentence for eight years but was paroled with help from the father when he became an adult. He is progressing well."

He concluded, "I know I've used extreme examples for this aspect of *staying curious*. Most of us don't face staying open and forgiving to such a degree, but you'll see it all as you support your brothers and sisters on Earth. A truly curious mind is open to growth, to learning, to understanding why people do what they do and to being influenced and guided by inspiration to help them as best we can. Judgment is saved for Father, who knows and understands each of us perfectly.

"By the way, we are taught to leave judgment in Father's hands. I think at a deeper level, He's also reminding us to be gentle with and not judge ourselves too harshly. When we understand what we're doing makes sense to us, we can challenge our own thinking and beliefs, be open to inspiration and love, and start to see things differently. That can help bring about healthier, long-lasting personal change.

"This is one of the reasons I told you at the outset of your training that this isn't as much about doing things differently, but rather, it's a way of being – *being present, being grateful,* a mindset of *moving forward* and one of *staying curious.* As we make those thought habits a way of being, our actions will naturally follow. *'For as he thinketh in his heart, so is he,'* [3] is a profound truth." He paused. "I can tell you're getting this. Let's go do some inspiring," Will said.

---

[3] PROVERBS 23:7

Chapter Fifteen

As the two finished many instances of encouraging others to *stay curious*, with Will leading the way they stepped from a portal onto a hill overlooking a large body of water. The side on which they were standing had green grass with lots of trees, the shoreline below with gentle slopes of sand. In contrast, across the water were barren hills, the coastline of the lake jagged and covered with boulders. Overall, the climate felt hot and desert-like.

"This is the Sea of Galilee, as it looked at the time of Christ." Will explained.

Jeff did a slow, full 360. "Wow, I never thought I'd get to see this. This is holy ground." They stood there quietly soaking it in, imagining what it was like when He was there.

Will finally broke the silence. "You'll understand soon why we're here. For now, let's debrief our adventure."

They plopped down on the ground and Jeffrey began.

"It felt good encouraging people to *stay curious*, to keep learning and have a growth mindset. I got a kick out of that group of men in their 90's taking classes together at the university. They were really smart guys who still wanted to keep learning. We didn't even need to influence them. They were great examples of staying curious."

"There are times I wish I could get on the world's largest microphone and tell all the youth of the world, in fact, tell *everyone* that learning is a lifelong opportunity – that once one gets to the point of knowing it all, it's time to learn something new," chimed in Will.

Jeffrey nodded and went on, "It was interesting to see how *staying curious* played out at work. I'd seen elements of *'that's how we've always done it,' 'we've tried that,'* and *'that won't work here,'* at the company where I was employed, but didn't know it was that common everywhere else. Helping leaders be open to other possibilities felt like we might actually be contributing to people's livelihoods. Related to that was inspiring people to come up with a new or different way of doing something, which could lead to new inventions and more businesses. There was more application of angel traits in the workplace than I would have thought.

"As you said, there were so many dimensions to staying curious," Jeff went on. "It was interesting how many people seem quick to be offended. Sometimes someone said or did something that was deliberately meant to offend, but that was the exception. Most of the time, people heard or took something the wrong way. *Staying curious* helped some work through it rather quickly.

"Sometimes it seemed oddly like they wanted to be offended. I found that curious in and of itself. They were offended by something that wasn't intended, distanced themselves from that person or lashed out and things spiraled down from there. When people stayed genuinely curious and sought to understand each other, the outcome was always more productive. I'm grateful some heard that message.

"Speaking of gratitude, I think staying curious also ties to other angel traits," Jeffrey continued. "The more we're aware of and grateful for all the blessings surrounding us, the more we want to deepen our understanding and learn about them. And in relation to being present, my favorite encounters were those where people had rushed to judgment about someone. If we could get them to back up, stay curious and really listen to understand, they were able to move forward together and have a better outcome."

"We're getting to the point where you won't need much more tutoring my friend," observed William. "I too really enjoyed the peace that seemed to come over people as they responded to our promptings of *'stay curious.'* You can see it in their eyes when they let go of judgment or defensiveness and open their minds to the possibilities.

"Jeffrey, we've finished our initial exploration of the angel traits. You know by now we will continue to gain deeper insights as we stay open and curious to learn more. These four lay a foundation for our progress and for helping others. Before we experience the fifth, this is a good moment to pause and answer questions you might have. Anything come to mind?"

Jeffrey reflected on what he'd gone through since his arrival in the world of spirits, including his visits to Earth. He was struck by the contrast of the two worlds.

"If I'd known how remarkable the spirit world is, I would have been anxious to get here, rather than fearing death. I think everyone would. It's good Father doesn't reveal that or people might want to come here before their time. But why the contrast? Why is it part of God's plan that Earth life be so difficult?"

"It's an important question. First, remember the ultimate goal is to become more like Christ, to receive His eternal peace, happiness and joy. We achieve that through having an earthly experience, as He did, which includes overcoming temptation and enduring adversity by doing the will of the Father. It was necessary for our spirit to be clothed in a physical body, as was His, one that experiences pleasure and pain, health and sickness, appetites and passions, joy and sorrow. It is through experiencing those opposites, mastering those appetites and by obeying the commandments He's given for our progress and well-being that we grow the most, far beyond what we've ever dreamed or could have achieved by simply remaining spirits."

Will continued, "And yet mortals don't have to wait for those blessings. As we do our best to do God's will, including trusting His personal timeline for each of us, we can have the same inner peace on Earth as we have here. As we exercise faith and follow Father's commandments, we can experience joy that is that much sweeter *because* it's in the midst of tribulation. The more we strive to do that on Earth, the more depth of character we bring with us into the spirit world at Father's time for us, which better prepares us to continue to move forward.

"This also ties to our angel traits. If while on Earth we always yearn for something else, something better, at the expense of being fully present with life, we don't learn gratitude for God's current blessings, including those that come through adversity. As we exercise faith and trust in God's perfect knowledge, He will magnify and bless our efforts in the moment, then help us move forward to this stage of our progress when it's best for us, according to His eternal wisdom and love. Remember, Christ didn't avoid pain and suffering. He willingly descended below all things, yet found and continues to have perfect joy in love and service. Like

Him, our opportunity is to experience and share love wherever we are and in whatever circumstances.

"I know that's a lot to ponder. There's more to discuss along those lines, and we'll do so later. Right now, a very special event is about to begin that will tie into what you're asking. You've successfully internalized four angel traits – *be present, be grateful, move forward,* and *stay curious*. Now we add a fifth. You'll recall I said this one isn't as much a trait as a powerful message, the most important I can think of."

Suddenly, flashes of light brought other spirits, including Jeffrey's mother, to the hillside. As more arrived, they hugged each other without saying much, maintaining a reverence as they gathered. Soon about thirty spirits were sitting on the ground together. There was a large flash of light nearby and without anyone saying anything, they all stood together clearly out of respect for this visitor.

"This is the Apostle Peter," Will said to Jeffrey, as they both rose.

"*The* Apostle Peter, as in the one who personally knew Christ?!" Jeffrey asked under his breath.

"One and the same," Will responded.

Peter sat on a smooth boulder and signaled for them to sit. Everyone got comfortable. He didn't say anything at first, just smiled and looked around at the group, making eye contact with each one. Then this special witness of Christ began.

"I am so grateful to be with you, to share some thoughts from my heart." He paused at length, still looking deliberately at each person, nodding recognition when he spotted William who nodded and smiled back.

This beloved disciple of the Savior then tenderly continued.

"The Holy Scriptures, those accounts of all my brethren, are true. We are witnesses of our Master's life, death and resurrection. Looking back, I think those of us who recorded those events focused on our Savior's words and actions as He taught, blessed, healed and ultimately sacrificed for us. We wanted to get the facts and teachings right, as witnesses of this eternally significant event. What I want to convey to you now however, is how it *felt* when we were with Him. I learned as much or more just being in His presence as I did from the words He spoke. It is what I *felt* from Him that was truly life changing.

"The first few miracles of healing we witnessed, I focused on the person who had been healed, hardly able to believe my eyes. I would look close to see if leprosy was actually gone, to test if a blind person could really see or wait to see if a crippled man, who was now walking, would falter.

"After seeing more of these miracles, and after my faith in Him deepened, I started instead watching the Lord. The joy that filled His countenance when He healed someone was profound. He often teared up as he smiled, and that was whether that person remembered to thank Him or not. He delighted in healing bodies and souls. I could tell He truly and deeply loved everyone He touched.

"But the strongest recollection of my feelings at that time relate to His resurrection." Peter paused, then said with absolute conviction, "We saw, spoke with, touched and even embraced our risen Lord several times after his crucifixion. One of the most memorable moments for me was when He visited us in a small room where the windows and doors were locked. We'd barricaded ourselves in for fear of being arrested and killed as Jesus had been. Then, suddenly, there He was standing in the center of the room. At first we thought we were seeing a ghost, but as Jesus visited with us, ate with us and let us see and feel the wounds in His hands, feet and side, our initial astonishment was replaced by overwhelming joy and gratitude. We realized that truly this was our Redeemer. This was He who had literally, physically risen from the dead. Jesus had foretold this several times, but we hadn't comprehended what He was saying.

"When our Savior first appeared, we were terrified. In response, He very lovingly said, *'Peace be unto you,'* and that's exactly what we felt. At a moment when we should have felt panic, confusion and fear, each of us to a person mentioned later that he felt absolute peace and pure love.

"We visited throughout the evening. I noticed He deliberately spent time with each of us. At one point, He called me by name, took me to His side and let me know how much He appreciated and loved me."

Peter now had his eyes closed as he replayed the scene. "I will never as long as I exist, forget His loving smile at that moment. When he smiled at me, I felt a warmth through my body…through my entire soul…that I could never describe. You've all had a taste of it as you entered the spirit world and yet what we feel here is the faintest shadow to experiencing His love in person. I recount the words of my dear friend Paul, who later wrote, *'I am persuaded that neither death, nor life, nor angels, nor principalities, nor powers, nor things present, nor things to come, nor height, nor depth, nor any other creature, shall be able to separate us from the love of God, which is in Christ Jesus our Lord.'*[4] That's how I felt when I saw the living Christ."

Peter concluded, "Remember, as you serve those on Earth or here in the world of spirits, you are serving Him and you are sharing a portion of His love to help our beloved brothers

---

[4] ROMANS 8:38-39

and sisters draw closer to Him, who is the ultimate Source of joy, peace and fulfillment. I leave my love and deepest gratitude with you all."

He finished his remarks, and all stood. Peter went around and gave each spirit a long, warm hug; the light around each increasing brightly as he did so. After hugging Jeffrey, he pulled back a bit, placed his hands on both shoulders, looked directly into his eyes, smiled and said, "I understand you're a good student. Take what you're feeling now, what I felt from our Savior, and share this message far and wide."

He then leaned forward and whispered something in Jeffrey's ear – something he felt throughout his entire soul, bringing immediate tears to his eyes. Peter turned, thanked the group again and was off in a bright flash of light. No one left immediately, all feeling profound gratitude for this special moment.

"Now for a critical part of your training," said William softly, finally breaking the silence. They both nodded to the rest of the group…and disappeared.

Chapter Sixteen

"As we embark on the last part of your training, there's something you need to see. I haven't shown you this yet, because I didn't want you distracted. I needed you fully focused on learning the first four traits," explained Will.

This sounds a bit mysterious thought Jeffrey. But he trusted his mentor completely, so he practiced what he'd just learned and remained curious.

Will continued, "Let's go back to that young woman who we saw praying so earnestly for help." In moments, they were back in the home they had visited previously.

The young woman was still clearly struggling, again praying, kneeling this time by a sofa in her living room. The TV across from her was on, but muted. It appeared she had been watching a show, was distracted by her worries and had dropped right there on her knees to continue pleading to God for help.

"Keep your eyes on her," said Will. He reached over and touched Jeffrey's temple with his forefinger. Immediately Jeffrey saw a being on the girl's sofa, legs folded, sitting directly in front of her. It was leaning over, talking quietly to her. It appeared to Jeffrey to have the form of a man, but something was off. More than what he was seeing, it was what Jeff felt that made him literally step back. There was such a feeling of…it was hard to describe… of darkness like a heavy fog coming from it, a feeling of evil, of negativity. It was as though it was sucking the energy right out of the room.

"Stay centered," Will calmly said. "Stay in touch with what you just felt as we listened to an Apostle of the Lord. You'll be fine."

Jeffrey took a deep breath and recalled that moving experience, which quickly settled him.

The being looked up at both of them. As it did, its eyes reflected Will and Jeffrey's light and like an animal in headlights, shone back in a weird, bright green color. Instead of being angry or surprised at their arrival, as Jeffrey thought it would be, it broke into a bright, toothy smile. It let out a strange laugh, then looked down and continued speaking quietly, but intensely to the young woman. This time, Jeffrey could hear what it was saying.

"You're useless, you know that. Why are you even praying? God doesn't care about you. There are so many more people out there that God really cares about. In fact, how do you

even know there is a God? What if that's a lie? Everyone has been lying to you lately. You can't trust anyone. God's existence could be the biggest lie of all. You might as well just die."

"No!" Jeff blurted out. The being looked up, startled at the outburst. "You're being lied to right now," insisted Jeffrey to the woman.

William looked at Jeffrey, put his hand on his shoulder and asked, "Based on what you are feeling right now; what you were feeling when you listened to an Apostle bear witness of Christ; based on what he whispered to you, Jeffrey; based on everything you've felt since you arrived in the spirit world, what do you want this struggling sister of yours to know?"

It all came together at that moment. With absolute clarity and confidence, Jeffrey stepped up behind the young woman. He was glowing brightly as he leaned over her smiling, tears streaming down his face, as he simply said, ***"You are loved."***

He paused. *"You…are…loved,"* Jeffrey slowly and deliberately repeated.

The demon cried out with anguish and left through the wall to go find another victim.

Both he and William watched as she took a deep breath, lifted her head, wiped her tears and went back up on the sofa. She sat there in silence, her face letting go of the strain. After a while she unmuted the set and continued watching a show. Then just minutes later fell sound asleep, her head tipping to the side as she sat upright.

"She'll struggle for a while, but for now she is feeling peace," said Will. "What you whispered to her and more importantly, what she felt as you did, opened her mind and heart to Father's spiritual confirmation that indeed she is loved – by God, by us and as you know now, by many others who are here to support her. It's a beautiful experience, isn't it?"

"Beyond words," replied Jeffrey softly. "But what was that thing? Was that what I think it was – a devil?"

"That's one of many names for it. In my role as an angel, I call them dimmers, because when they're successful, they take people's light away."

"Dimmers, huh?" Jeffrey nodded. "Very fitting. When I first saw it, I felt like it was sucking all the light and energy out of the room. I don't think I need to tell you; it actually scared me a bit."

"There's a reason for that, Jeffrey." Will paused. "What would you say is the opposite of love?"

"Hate," Jeffrey answered quickly.

"Consider the possibility that the opposite of love is fear. Fear drives many if not most negative emotions, including hate. When a parent yells at a child for running out into the street the outward emotion is anger, but it's fueled by fear that the parent could have lost the child in an accident.

"When someone is racist their ugly hatred is usually based on unfounded fears the person has developed over time that they are going to be hurt, lose their job or simply from fear of the unknown – of someone who is different than they are.

"When our Savior was born on Earth, the first words declared by angels were *'Fear not!'* This was not only to calm the quaking shepherds, but I believe, a hopeful proclamation to the entire world that the opposite of fear, the actual Source of pure love had just entered mortality. When we are fully centered in our faith in Christ there is indeed nothing to fear, whatever life throws our way. The dimmer was trying to instill fear into the young woman – fear that there might not be a God, that she isn't enough, that she is alone and above all, that she isn't loved.

"When you saw the dimmer and were afraid, which by the way is a natural reaction – so was I at first – it seemed to get stronger, a powerful, dark influence. But remember that they are never as powerful as we are, Jeffrey, as long as our faith is centered in Christ. He is our strength and our reason never to fear. That's why I waited until you'd strengthened your spiritual core before showing you the enemy."

"From the stories I recall in church, I would think we'd see legions of them. Why was there only one?" inquired Jeff.

"Sometimes you'll see them in numbers. Sometimes they're alone. There are times when the person we're helping has developed a strong thought habit that they are useless or not loved. In those cases, dimmers can focus their energy elsewhere. Those people beat themselves up enough that they don't need any 'help,'" explained Will. "Father makes sure no one is tempted or challenged beyond what they can overcome, however difficult at times it might seem. We help in our own way by being on the lookout for those who need that simple, powerful, eternal message of truth that *they are loved.*"

Jeff was deep in thought. After a long pause, he quietly said, "The greatest commandment is to love God, the second to love others as we love ourselves. As I grow in my love for others by *being present* and *staying curious,* not judging them will be easier, even spontaneous. When I feel *gratitude* for all of my blessings and acknowledge the Source of all that is good, I naturally feel love toward God. And when I humbly love myself, I care enough to *keep moving forward,* to serve others and to make the most of what Father has given me.

Love ties all the angel traits together. The more I stay in touch with the love I'm feeling now, I won't need to be commanded to love. I'll want to do so with every part of my being. It's truly all about love."

He paused again. "There's someone I need to go see," exclaimed Jeffrey.

"I know," replied Will. "I'll see you at your mother's home when you're ready. Remember that time passes differently here on Earth, much more quickly compared to the timelessness of the spirit world. Several Earth months have passed since your physical death. You'll catch on when you get to where you're going."

Jeffrey nodded. Just as they were about to depart, a flash of light appeared in the room and two people who looked like the young woman's grandparents stepped through a portal. They sat on each side of her and rested their hands on hers as she continued sleeping. They looked up at Will and Jeffrey and smiled. Jeff knew she would be in very loving hands.

The two smiled back, then left in different directions.

Chapter Seventeen

Jeff was headed to see Nick. He found him standing outside their friend Neil's home. The noise inside indicated that a party was going on. Jeffrey glanced through the wall and noted that many of his and Nick's friends were present, laughing and having a good time. Jeff watched as Nick paused, trying to get up the courage to ring the bell. After standing there for some time, Nick turned to leave. Jeff followed and lovingly said to his friend, *"Nick, be present. Quiet your mind. You know they'll love seeing you."*

Nick paused and turned back. He didn't ring the bell, just turned the handle and walked in. Andy and Craig were the first to see him.

"Nick! You made it! Great to see you!" Everyone else turned, shouting, "Nick!" It took only seconds before he was fully engaged in the party, guys slapping him on the back, someone bringing him a drink. Nick looked relieved, relaxed and happy. The tension and grief were gone from his face, and he seemed to be his old self. Jeff listened in as Nick later confided in a conversation with Neil, "I've been getting some help, and feel a lot better."

After staying close to Nick for a while, Jeffrey took time to focus on each person in the room, recounting memories and feeling gratitude for each of their influences and friendship in his life. Finally, he looked at Nick once again and knowing that he would keep close tabs on his best buddy, decided it was time for another visit.

∞∞∞

Jeffrey found Jake in bed, asleep in his new apartment. Jake had moved out of his dad's home and was on his own. Like Nick, he looked healthier and appeared to be doing well.

"I think you got over me a little too quickly," Jeffrey chided his younger brother, but he knew better. This had been a hard road for Jake, and he was just now getting his legs under him. Moving out on his own was a good first step.

Jeff took the opportunity to talk to Jake while he slept, thanking him through tears for being a great brother. He wished he'd done better at being a big brother, but somehow knew that all Jake felt for him was love and gratitude; so he was leaving with no regrets. He knew, as he knew with Nick, he'd stay close – that both he and his mom would.

"You make the most of your life," Jeff directed, as he wrapped things up. "And know that I will only be a thought away."

At that moment, a strong impression came to Jeffrey that their mother was in the room or was at least aware the two were together. He sensed she'd left him alone to visit with Jake but was clearly pleased her boys were doing well.

"I love you, mom," Jeff said out loud. "I love you both," he said emphatically. Jake suddenly lifted his head and looked around, clearly half asleep. He nodded, smiling as though he sensed something special was going on around him, muttered something completely unintelligible, then turned over and was out cold. Jeffrey repeated, "I love you both," then left the room for his final visit. On his way out Jeffrey quietly said, 'Thank you, Father."

The next one was tough – very tough. Even with all the love he'd felt in the spirit realm since his passing; even understanding the powerful traits Will had shared; even after visiting with a chosen servant of the Lord, Jeffrey was struggling to see his father. He'd done so many hurtful things over so many years, not only to him but especially to Jake. He knew he couldn't honestly say that he'd forgiven his dad, so it felt like a lie that he was going to reach out. Yet something deep inside said he needed to at least make the effort.

It was still nighttime, and his dad was already in bed. He stood over him, very nervous, not knowing quite what to say. It took a long time before Jeffrey broke the silence.

"Um, hi dad. I didn't plan what I was going to say to you. It just felt like I was supposed to come see you. I know you can't hear me…I don't think you can…but hopefully you can somehow feel what I have to say."

He paused and took a deep breath. "For so long, it's been just anger. I'm so mad at you. You betrayed me, you betrayed Jake, and you betrayed mom when you hurt us. You were supposed to be a loving dad. We needed you when mom died and you let us down. I've learned from Will…um…from an angel…that you were doing what made sense to you at the time, but that doesn't help very much. You still hurt us, and that's hard to forgive."

Jeff paused at length. "Here's all I can promise. I'll do my best to get over it and stay open…" There was another even longer pause, then he continued, "and, believe it or not, right now, I really do hope the best for you. I hope you're able to get your life in order. Get cleaned up, get close to Jake and be a dad, if he'll let you. I don't know. I hardly know what to say," Jeffrey was really struggling. "Just that I'll do my best, and hope you do, as well."

At that moment, something completely unexpected happened. Jeffrey's dad sat up in bed. He looked around bewildered, then locked in on Jeffrey standing next to him. Jeff noticed to his astonishment that his dad's body was still lying in bed with his eyes closed. It was his spirit that was now sitting upright.

"Jeff?!" his father exclaimed, clearly able to see him. "Jeffrey? Is that you?"

His father's spirit started to rise above the bed, leaving his mortal shell behind.

"Dad, I think you just died," said Jeffrey, in shock at what he was seeing.

"Jeffrey, I'm so very, very, sorry," was all his father was able to express. Just then, a light flashed in the room. Will appeared. He looked down and spoke directly to Jeff's father.

"Quinton, it's not your time yet. You need to go back into your body."

"Oh, please don't make me. This feels so amazing," Quint responded. "Please let me come with you. Please let me be with my son," he gestured to Jeffrey.

"You'll be reunited soon enough. You have another son with whom you need to heal, and much progress to make before you can pass over. It won't be easy. You'll have to work hard and keep *moving forward* but loved ones on this side will be supporting you. You won't be alone. When you awake, you'll think this was a dream. Hopefully it will be enough to nudge you forward. Go back now," Will commanded.

Jeffrey's dad looked over at him with tears in his eyes. He started to say something else, but bowed his head, then leaned back and settled down into his body. Will stepped over, placed his hands just over Quinton's head and gave him an angelic blessing. Just as he said, "Amen," Quinton gasped loudly. He sat up, coughing and gasping for air. He clutched at his chest with one hand, grabbing his phone and dialing 911 with the other.

"I think I'm having a heart attack!" he yelled. "Please come quickly."

Jeffrey and Will stayed until paramedics had taken Jeff's father off in an ambulance.

"Wow, that was unexpected!" Jeff exclaimed. "I'm guessing you knew that would happen?"

"Yes, I knew. Just as I knew you'd want to see Jake, Nick and even your dad when you were feeling such profound love. I appreciate your honesty with your dad. Forgiveness doesn't usually happen quickly. Many times, we need to dig deep. It's a spiritual blessing that ultimately comes from Father, but it does come as we do our best to *stay curious*, to serve others and to draw closer to the Savior – the ultimate Source of love, understanding and forgiveness. I'm proud of you and really respect how you handled this with your father."

"Now, Jeffrey, I have something for you to do."

Chapter Eighteen

Jeffrey stepped through a portal and was standing over a developing scene on Earth. He was looking at what clearly had been a bad car accident. He watched the chaos below as people were running to help. Some were frantically trying to get car doors open, others scrambled to call 911, as other onlookers gathered at corners of the intersection. It appeared two mangled cars were involved. They must have hit with tremendous force, their front ends meshed almost as one. Steam from one car was shooting upward. Jeffrey could hear people screaming inside.

His attention was drawn to a young man sitting in the passenger seat of one of the cars, his eyes closed, his head leaning to the side against a smashed window. The young man's spirit suddenly sat upright, his mortal head still leaning against the window fragments. The young man rose out of his body, through the roof and over the car. He watched as they finally got the door open and pulled his limp body out. One woman quickly determined that the young man wasn't breathing and started to try to resuscitate him there in the street while other onlookers helped the other passengers. The young man tried to assure his rescuer that he was okay – that he actually felt fine.

Just then, the young man looked over at Jeffrey who had slowly descended to his side.

He froze, surprised to see this heavenly being. It took him a moment to gather his thoughts, but then he quietly ventured a question, "Are…are you an angel?"

Jeffrey smiled. "You can call me that."

∞∞∞

Approximately two Earth years after Jeff visited his father in his bedroom, a beautiful picture of his dad appeared on Jeffrey's gratitude wall.

(NOT) THE END

A Note from the Author

Is this a true story?

As I completed this book, I was tempted to add to the title, *"Based on true events."* I believe it would have been justifiable to do so. Consider the following:

Near Death Experiences

Hundreds, if not thousands of "near death experiences" or NDE's have been recorded over many decades. My first exposure to these was through Dr. Raymond Moody's book, <u>Life After Life</u>[5], in which he documented many of these accounts. Dr. Moody had been capturing NDE's from patients in the U.S. for many years while unbeknownst to him, Dr. Elizabeth Kubler Ross was hearing similar experiences from her many patients in Switzerland. When the two met at a conference and compared notes of what they had discovered independent of each other, the overlapping evidence was remarkable. Since then, many other books and articles have been written that reinforce hope of life after death. As a Christian with my faith in a resurrection, I hold this belief deeply, but even from a scientific, research-based approach, the evidence of life after death is compelling.

---

[5] Life After Life, Dr. Raymond A. Moody, Harper One, 2015

The Messiah

As George Frideric Handel composed the musical masterpiece, "Messiah," in 1741, he didn't leave his home for twenty-three days, asking his servant to bring meals to his room. As recorded in one of the album's liner notes, *"We know that Handel was deeply moved during the 23 days. At one point, after having written down the Hallelujah Chorus, he called to his manservant and with eyes filled with tears, exclaimed, 'I did think I did see all heaven before me, and the Great God himself.'"*[6]

The account of William and Jeffrey watching as a heavenly orchestra and choir of angels reveal "Messiah" to a composer on another world is of course, purely my imagination. As I have listened with tears to that inspiring composition, as well as other magnificent pieces from other composers, and believing that God's creations extend far beyond our realm and limited thinking, I've wondered if perhaps, Father shares some of His children's most remarkable creations, especially tributes to His Beloved Son, with those on other worlds. It is at the very least, an interesting possibility. The fact that Handel felt divinely guided to compose it is documented.

---

[6] Jay Welch, George Frideric Handel "Messiah," The Philadelphia Orchestra, The Mormon Tabernacle Choir, Columbia Masterworks

Angel Traits

I've had the wonderful opportunity for the past thirty-plus years to work for a leadership consulting firm, specializing in shaping corporate culture. Part of what we do (very effectively, I might add) is to help leaders and employees throughout our client organizations operate at their best, so they can achieve better and more sustainable results. Though I have reframed related concepts through my own grounding and understanding, the angel traits I've shared parallel principles I've seen hundreds of thousands of people employ successfully, both at work and at home. Traits like *being present, staying curious, moving forward, gratitude* and even *self-reflection* are just some of those that have certainly had an impact on my own life as well. Since this is a faith-based book, I want to be clear that the company I work for is not a religious organization – they are a secular consulting firm that has worked with leaders of Fortune 500 companies and many others around the globe. However, it is easy for me personally to see elements of similar life-changing concepts in a religious framework, because of their proven, remarkable impact on individuals and their families.

Personal Stories

Some of the experiences I've shared are my own. For example, the Spirit whispering to Jeffrey at the funeral that there is indeed a spirit in each of our mortal bodies reflects an insight I received while in a college anatomy lab studying a cadaver. I believe as we each pray for answers and ponder eternally significant questions, Father will reveal truths to each of us that are profound, including that He is real, and we are indeed His beloved children.

Some experiences I shared in the chapters on *"go forward"* and *"stay curious,"* were those of friends and associates I've known over the years who inspired me through their strength and resilience.

One particular example worth noting is a dear friend of mine, F. Enzio Busche, who died twice and was told to return each time to this life. As he shared both accounts, he tearfully told me the message he took away each time was that it is all about love – that he felt he could almost "breathe love" in the spirit world. Enzio has done a remarkable job of carrying that message throughout the world. He passed away a few years ago and was allowed to stay this time. I miss him but am confident that he continues to share that message boldly and lovingly throughout the spirit world.

The Savior

Most importantly, the statement "based on a true story" relates to our Savior, Jesus Christ. He is everything to me – the Source of creation, redemption, atonement, and The One who embodies perfect love.

Despite the above real experiences, because this is a work of fiction and because I didn't want to mix important eternal truths with what is also fantasy (the fun I had imagining different aspects of Paradise like food pods, portals, gratitude walls and such), I left "based on true events" off at the beginning. But what if much of it is true? What are the implications, the possibilities and what are we each doing to prepare now for that next inevitable stage in our journey?

I hope this work has provided insights from the afterlife through the fictional training of a heavenly being. Which begs the question as to whom I'm referring. Is that heavenly being an angel, Jeffrey, you as the reader, or all of the above? Something I invite you to ponder.

About the Author

John McKay has been a leadership consultant for over thirty-five years specializing in helping leaders, teams and organizations around the world perform more consistently at their best. He earned a bachelor's degree in political science from the University of Utah and a Master of Business Administration from the Anderson Graduate School of Management at UCLA. Most importantly, John is a husband, father and grandfather. In these different roles and now through writing, John hopes to continue to fulfill his own purpose: *"To inspire a positive, meaningful and lasting difference in the lives of my family and throughout the world."*

Check out John's podcast on "How to know there's a God" and "Developing a meaningful relationship with God" at http://findinggodslove.org

Made in the USA
Coppell, TX
15 August 2023